Chronicles of Existence:
Earth One

Armin M. Borgia

ISBN-13: 978-1644400968

DEDICATION

My ex-wife for forcing me into solitude which created the basis for this story. Jared for starting this journey with me. Anderson for the guidance. Mariah for thoughtful feedback. Patty for all the support to get to this point.

ACKNOWLEDGMENTS

Thanks to TimidPunk for the amazing artwork. Seeing these characters come to life on paper has been one of the coolest parts so far. Thanks to anyone who read the story and gave me the hope to make it possible. Thanks to Michelle for really making this possible by giving me life and nurturing my freaky imagination.

PROLOGUE: GERMANY PART I

Seated within his mobile command tent, Hans was less than thrilled with his current, and uncomfortable, situation. The leather of his boots was stiff from the cold Hungarian winter and the grove of trees surrounding the camp did little to protect them from the bitter winds. He had been handpicked by the Wehrmacht HQ for this mission, but he'd put in to be considered so he couldn't blame anyone but himself for being here. While attempting to prep his pistol with cold fingers, he silently cursed this frozen wasteland and his thoughts began to drift back home to Berlin. He missed the cozy stone fireplace in his flat and all the beautiful young German girls so willing to serve the Reich.

He'd be back in his warm flat with all his girls soon enough. Currently, he had more pressing matters to attend to. Matters that required all of his focus. Before he had left the Rhineland, Hans was told this was a key offensive for the Third Reich; maybe the last key offensive of the war. He'd planned the best maneuver he could with the troops he was given. The General in charge, Josef Dietrich, had just simply nodded as Hans explained his battle strategy to him. Few words had exchanged since that meeting. The General's stern demeanor was as cold as the winter wind and Hans wasn't sure if it was him he appeared to be bored with or just how he was normally.

Hans bounces back to reality and after peaking at his watch, realizes the hour he had been dreading all morning had finally come. He was to join the General outside to observe the beginning of the strike. He was as ready as he ever would be, so bracing himself for the inevitable cold, he marched outside to find the General.

As Hans stepped into the motorcade, he spotted the General perched atop a small hill overlooking the camp. He hiked himself up the mound and stopped to stand next to him. Hans and the General surveyed the camp in silence as their force checked ammo stores and equipment. Hans counted 8 Panzers in the formation and he knew they had about 1,200 men in this attachment. He'd seen on a report that the full strength of the German force was well over 400,000. "Ich hoffe für diese Kampagne" (I'm hopeful for this campaign) The General says, breaking the silence. Hans turned toward the massing Red Army and a shiver ran down his spine. He had his doubts but did not dare to voice them.

The General abruptly turns and starts to walk higher up the mound, leaving Hans standing by himself. Feeling like everyone was looking at him as if he was incompetent, Hans smoothly turns and follows, only seconds later. Once at his side again, Hans is startled as the General screams the forward order. This was a fantastic spot to view their troops march out and meet the Red Army surrounding the lake. With Panzers leading the way, they watched as the clean snow turned to muddy tracks as their garrison met the larger German force massing outside of camp. The battle plans they'd drafted had the forces split around the lake creating a spearhead to assault the Russian troops waiting on the other side. Hans anxiously watched from his perch as the maneuver began and was quickly brought to a standstill by heavy counter fire. Out of the corner of his eye, he noticed the General leaving the mound, headed for the command tent. He leered over the battle once more before he followed.

Days had passed since the strike began and their forces were still under fire by Russian artillery. A gut-wrenching panic overcame Hans. He felt reassured in his panic as stone faced Dietrich was also stressing in the tent. "Diese Kampagne wird scheitern und in diesem Tempo wird das Lager in einer Angelegenheit von Tagen überschritten werden. Was sollen wir machen? (This campaign will fail and at this rate, the camp will be overrun in a matter of days. What should we do?) The fear in his heart snuck into his throat, stealing his breath and shaking his words. The General's eyes gazed over to him. The fear in him didn't show at this moment. "Wir müssen ein Wort nach Berlin schicken und auf weitere Anweisungen warten "(We must send word to Berlin and await further instructions.) The calm authority in his voice left no room for arguments.

The General made haste to the telephone machine while Hans stood by, peaking out the door. With a final twist of the dial, the machine opened a line to Berlin. Hans paced nervously from one end of the tent to the other awaiting someone to connect. The sounds of artillery fire growing ever louder meant the battle was getting closer to camp. After only a few seconds that dragged like hours, the General perked up as someone at command began to speak to him. The General covers the receiver with his hand and whispers to Hans "Sie haben mich warten Jemand wichtig ist, mit uns zu sprechen" (They have me waiting. Someone important is looking to speak with us.) Hans tiptoes closer to the General as a voice comes through the phone. "Mein Freund is this Josef Dietrich?" Stone faced as ever, he replied "Ja das ist. Ich bin hier bei Hans Lorenz. Wem spreche ich mit?" (Yes, this is. I'm here with Hans Lorenz. Whom am I speaking with?) The man on the other end of the phone quietly tells him in English, "This is Adolf Hitler. I need you to listen to me carefully. The war is over. Take this time, if you can, to flee." The look of sheer terror on the General's face drew Hans to come even closer. "All will be explained later but please leave your current position and meet me in Budapest at April's end. You'll find a bunker hidden among ruins or a monastery on the southern tip of Margaret Island. The only souls who know of it will meet us there. Access the bunker by pressing in the middle of the sundial." He opens his mouth to reply but doesn't have a chance before the voice speaks again. "Also, use English and hide your heritage. It will save your life. They're coming for me. I must go for now, but I hope to see you both alive and well in Budapest. Please be cautious. Auf Wiedersehen." The line goes dead. Josef hung the receiver up and at a snail's pace, found a nearby box to sit on.

Hans kept his distance but breaks the silence. "Was haben sie gesagt, General? Was sollen wir tun?" (So, what did they say General? What are we to do?) Regaining some composure, he replied in English, "Call me Josef." He stands and straightens his outfit for a moment. Hans is just looking at him, waiting for him to continue. "Josef?" He prods. "Oh" Josef says. "That was Herr Hitler. We're to abandon camp because we've lost the war. He wants us to meet him in Budapest." Hans looked at the General in disbelief. "Sag mir die Wahrheit." Josef points to himself. "Do I look like a story teller Lorenz?" He asks. "He also said to use English and hide the fact we're German." Hans sits his rear onto a desk next to him. "But why would Herr Hitler speak to you? What do you make of this?" Hans stutters. "It's a way out of the hole we've found ourselves in. Pack your bag. Now. We're leaving." Hans stands. "We're taking the Tatra. You've got mere minutes. That battle will be here soon." Hans nods and quickly finds himself on the move to his tent. He didn't feel in control of his body, rather it was just moving. His important items found their way into a bag and with it slung up over his shoulder, he headed out toward the truck.

As he lobs his bag into the cab, a mortar crashes into the ground too close for comfort. In a split second of clarity before it detonated, his life flashed before him. The oddity of this day finally set in as the mortar triggered, throwing Hans back off his feet. His body slammed the ground hard as mounds of dirt and debris rained over the area, covering him. Before his mind could process what had happened, the cold dirt he lay in turned into a soft cloth seat. The deep roar of the diesel engine filled the cabin as he regained his wits and realized he was in the truck. He whipped his head around to the driver's seat and was relieved to see Josef steering. "Sit up and fasten yourself; we're not out of danger yet."

Still reeling from the shock, Hans slowly twists his body upright and fastened his safety belt. Another explosion rocked the truck from behind causing Hans to peer through the back window. He could barely see through the smoke, but soldiers were becoming visible through the tree line. The national emblem affixed to the jackets was noticeable which gave him some relief. "These are our men." He told Josef as he turned back around. "This escape seems to be a success." Hans braces himself against the dash as the truck launches off of a small hill into a large muddy hole. Josef expertly maneuvers through the mud and brings the truck back onto solid land. Hans hides his panic well. "We will find out soon enough." Josef replies as he shifts into a higher gear, speeding away from the last battle of the war and the end of the Nazi machine.

As they drove, the battle sounds became nonexistent. The silence fed to the worry now building in Hans. They were deep in enemy controlled territory and had nearly 500km to cross without being captured. "So, what do we do now?" Hans said aloud, not necessarily waiting for a response. "Get rid of this truck and these uniforms before we're discovered" Josef replied anyway. "We'll need to blend in if we want to make it to Budapest alive".

The rough terrain finally turned to road and the truck smoothly passed over the gravel. Hans silently praised this. After a few moments of bliss, Josef begins to downshift, and the truck eventually jerks to a halt. He opens the door and with his foot on the seat, looks both directions before sitting back down and slamming the door closed. He looks sideways at Hans and cracks the slightest smirk before announcing "Hang on, this is going to be bumpy." Hans had to double take. This is the first time he had ever seen Josef smile. What was he about to do? Revving the engine, Josef drops the shifter into first gear and begins moving the truck forward. He jerks the wheel to the right and aims the truck to enter the woods along the road. Hans was thankful he was fastened as the truck bounced through the brush. As the truck continued through the forest, Hans noticed Josef's smirk turn into a full-on smile. He seemed to be enjoying himself. What an odd time to be having fun he thought. Brushing it off, his gaze focused back forward, and an immediate bout of panic hit him. The ground seemed to end ahead. He braced the best he could as the truck careened off the edge and crashed into a small ravine. It only appeared to be a few meters deep, but the initial panic still had his heart beating fast. Josef lets out a quiet giggle as he hangs in his seat. Hans couldn't help but join him. Loud belly laughs filled the cabin. The laughing quieted after both men had a solid bout and

Josef looks over to Hans. "Let's get what supplies we can salvage and hide the truck. It'll give us a good head start."

Driving through the forest knocked loose plenty of brush, which made the task of covering the truck fairly easy. Once the truck was sufficiently hidden, the food stores were raided before the men hiked back to the road. They had covered themselves in blankets to hide the uniforms and bags until they could get other provisions to blend in better. Josef pulled a compass out of his pocket and spun in place until he found east. "We'll follow this road here to find Budapest, to the east." He tells Hans. He nods in agreement before the men begin their march to safety.

Hours and miles passed as they walked with a purpose. Josef's pace was quick, and Hans's calves were on fire. It was now near the end of midday and the air was beginning to chill. Breathing was starting to hurt as the air turned and Hans was worried they'd have to camp outside tonight. Attempting to take his mind off the cold, he thought how lucky they were that not a soul had passed since they began the journey. "I hope we come across a dwelling soon." Hans says aloud. "We need to get out of these uniforms and we may freeze to death with no shelter." He shivered as he spoke. Josef replies while continuing to walk. "It's been silent for a long while. Do you hear that now?" He stopped walking and held his arm out for Hans to also stop. A beautiful silence covers the area but is broken by a faint noise on the horizon. "I hear a home. Children's laughter." Josef told him. "We're close to something and I've got an idea" Hans listened intently while trying not to focus on his freezing extremities. "If anyone asks, we're headed to Budapest to meet our cousin. She has just delivered a baby" He suggested. "How's your Hungarian?" Hans asks. "Jobb, mint az unokatestvére baba" (Better than your cousin's baby) rolls off Josef's tongue like he had been born in Hungary. Hans could have sworn he saw the slightest smile grace Josef's face before he turned and began walking again. Hans followed, hoping they would be welcome in this home for the night.

Freezing rain began to fall as they continued traveling along the dirt road. They rounded a corner and the home they had heard a few moments ago came into view. A quaint group of squares build into a shelter. Hans was used to a little more luxury but wasn't going to make a fuss about anything offering him solace from this cold and soggy existence. He offended himself slightly by his initial reaction. They were in no position to be picky. Hans reiterated this to himself as they closed in on the home. One of the young girls spotted the pair and shrieked before running into the house screaming "Papa, papa." The other children followed suit and high tailed it into the house. Hans smirked as he asked Josef "Warm welcome thus far, huh?" Josef hid his smirk by shaking his head at the young man's joke.

Before they reached the door to knock, a middle-aged man with thick stubble and a stained white tank top stepped outside and trained a double barrel shotgun in their direction. Neither moved. "Hallottuk a csatát. (We heard the battle). Nem akar semmilyen baj. (Don't want any trouble.) Hans looks to Josef. He very calmly asks "Beszélsz angolul? (Do you speak English?). The man lets out a deep belly laugh, showing his missing or rotten teeth. "Well of course we do. It's the new thing these days." He drops the gun. Hans' sigh of relief is audible. "Here I was worried you two were Nazis. Coming to steal my family." He laughs loudly again. "I am Aron." He introduced himself. "Come get warm in my home. Come, Come." The man opens the door and holds it for them. Josef looks to Hans and shrugs before making his way into the home. With nothing to lose and daylight fading, Hans follows.

Aron closed the door behind Hans after he crossed the threshold. The smell of good beef stock tickled his nose. "What is that amazing smell? Soup?" Hans asked Aron. Josef smirked. "Yes! It is. Adel is making porkolt, err, meat stew. Fresh potatoes, cabbage…" He trailed off as he walked out of the room. Hans noticed one of the children peeking around the corner at the two men. An adult woman, Adel he assumed, carrying a basket of vegetables nearly tripped on the child and scolded them in her native language. The child ran away, and the woman smiled as she entered the room. Her smile is much more pleasant than Aron's he thinks to himself. "Please sit" She says to them as she offers with an open hand a couple of seats. Josef makes his way over to a seat near the fire. He sits hard, his joints still stiff from the cold. Hans moves toward the fire but continues to stand. Aron can be heard elsewhere in the small house, yelling at the children by what Hans could hear and understand. As Adel removes the cover from the pot over the fire, the small room becomes full of the aroma of the rich beef broth boiling in the pot. The rations they'd been living on for the past few weeks were nothing like this. His stomach growls loudly and Adel giggles. "The food should be ready very shortly." She told him. "Let me get you some of Aron's old clothes to change into. You must be freezing!" She stirred the pot once more before replacing the cover and exiting the room. Hans' gaze followed her body as she moved.

A sharp elbow to the thigh brought him back from his daze. "She is cute, huh?" Josef asked him. "You don't know the dynamic yet, don't get us killed." His stone-faced demeanor returned as he told Hans this. "She might be his. Be careful until we know." Hans nodded in agreement. This wasn't the first time he'd felt the longing for a warm woman he thought, but it was now something potentially attainable. He dropped his bottom onto the seat next to Josef while trying to control his thoughts. He'd work on her as the night went on, but they had to focus on hiding their true selves until this situation fully played out. He was able to relax before Aron stomped back into the room, followed by the children.

He points to the girl on the far left and begins "This is my oldest, Dorika" he lovingly tells the story. "This is my strong boy Jakab" He told as he pointed to the little boy who was no more than three years of age. With his hand on the final child's shoulder, he tells them "This is Margita. She lost her parents in this nonsense fighting. The same for Adel. I let them stay because a full home is a happy home. Happy is good for me since my wife passed." Hans noticed Aron get lost in memories as Adel strolled back into the room. It was confirmed though, he thought, Adel wasn't Aron's wife. He flashed her a smile as she passed by and she returned one filled with feeling and passion. The ideas he had repressed all flowed back. He would have her tonight. That much was certain.

Adel throws some clothes into their laps. "You'll find some privacy in this room." Her finger pointing to a doorway behind where she stood. "Go change! Dinner is nearly ready." Aron comes back from his memory trip to add "Yes, you don't want to miss this. Go change!" Without further prodding, the men stood and filed toward the room. As Hans was about to walk through the doorway, Adel stops him. She passed him another shirt but ran her hand up his thigh and over his cock in the same motion. He instantly gets hard. "I'll come see you later" she whispers to him before returning to the cooking pot.

He watched her strut back to the fire before Josef reached out and yanked him into the room.

"Hurry and get out of your German attire." Josef whispers. "Put it into this bag" He passes him a burlap sack. "We'll burn it later, once Aron has gone to sleep." He took a moment to compute the plan in his brain before he wiggled out of the uniform and stuffed it into the sack. Lost in thought, his raging erection slipped his mind until Josef pointed it out. "I appreciate the salute but that's not the kind I normally receive" he said with a smirk. It took a few seconds for Hans to get what he said but once he did, he quickly grabbed ahold of his cock, and lost his balance causing him to fall backward. Josef let out an audible laugh. Aron's footsteps began to close in and Hans covered his exposed privates as he popped his head in the door. "Everything ok in here?" He asked. Josef laughed a moment longer before responding "Oh yes, my brother here just fell over taking his boot off. No problems." Aron let out his loud, distinct laugh. "Ok great. Now hurry, hurry!" He says before returning to the other room. Josef chuckles again while he removes his uniform and puts it into another sack. "Keep that thing tame for now." He told him. "She'll get it later, I'm sure, but that guy might hurt you if he suspects anything. He's friendly enough but don't push it." Hans, defeated, stands while tucking in his hard dick between his legs. He quickly places on the clothes given to them and stands proud once he's fully clothed. "I'll have you know, she's teasing me. And it's been a while." Hans laughs. He plants himself on the bench to slide his boots back on. "Oh, don't I know it," Josef replies. "I'm a tad jealous but you can have her. I'll keep my eyes open for another opportunity." He sits next to him. "We've just been extremely lucky with this up to now, I want to keep the luck going." Hans stands and wiggles to settle the new clothing on his body. "I know Josef, I know. I'm not egging it on. I'm just going with it." Josef stands and does a similar wiggle to settle himself. "Great. Let's get back out there and eat. Keep the bag close. We'll burn it later." He snagged the sack and followed Josef out into the main room.

Adel was sitting toward the doorway with her skirt hiked up, secretly showing her pussy to the men as they walked out. With a quick whip of her hand, she fixed her dress as Aron and the children stalked back into the room. "You two look great!" He shouts. "Warm and dry now?" He asks. Quickly sitting to hide his constantly hard dick of late, Hans replies "Yes, I am. Thank you very much." Josef took a seat next to him near the fire. "We can't thank you enough for your hospitality." He told the room. Aron laughs his loud belly laugh. "Tell me about you my friends!" Hans looked to Josef. "We're Austrian farmers. Our cousin has had a baby. We're on our way to Budapest to meet them." He says, keeping details to a minimum. "Oh, what a wonderful reason to travel! Terrible time of year but wonderful reason. Adel! Feed these men. They're starving and cold!" Aron shouts. "Sit children. Eat too. Get big and strong." He sits down hard next to Hans on the bench. A stack of bowls near the fire were filled and divvied out amongst the room. Warm beef broth filled the air as the bowls were passed around. Once everyone in the room had a bowl, Aron pipes up "Everyone take hands." They all do as instructed and place the bowls down before interlocking their hands. Aron prays "Bless us, oh Lord, and these your gifts which we are about to receive from your bounty. Through Christ our Lord, Amen." The room repeats "Amen" and eagerly retrieves their food. Hans hadn't unlocked his eyes from Adel's since he sat. Their connection was becoming electric and Hans was having trouble focusing on anything else. The rest of the room was occupied by Aron's tale of his grandfather and his magic cabbage. Josef noticed but was the only one who seemed to. He figured it was because he was on high alert. Relaxing a little, he listened in on Aron's tale and chuckled a few times at the adventures of his kin.

The tale was long and the children became sleepy. Josef looked back and saw that Adel had found her way closer to Hans but was still being covert about it. "Time to rest family!" Aron shouts as he stands from his chair. Slowly, the children stand and file into the darkness of the other room. "You two can sleep in the room you changed. You'll find blankets and pillows in there." Adel stands and began to clean up from dinner. "We have you for breakfast before you leave?" Aron asks of the two. "That would be wonderful" Hans replied as he stood. "Yes, it will make the journey much more pleasant. Thank you." Josef adds, standing himself. "Sleep well friends" Aron shared before leaving the room for the night. Josef waited a moment, checking to make sure the coast was clear. "Don't be all night. We need our rest." He tells Hans and Adel before retiring into their room, smirking the whole way.

Grabbing his hand, Adel dragged Hans to the far corner of the main room. Behind a curtain, a small room was set up. "This is my room. Close to the cooking but far from everyone else." She smiles. He wasn't sure if he'd gone soft at all since he changed but he noticed how hard he was right now. "I'm leaving in the morning. Does that bother you?" He asked as she pushed him down on to the bed. "That doesn't change how I feel right now. You're a nice boy, I can tell." She unbuttons her dress near her neck and the entire thing drops to her feet. "I washed up for you earlier. Will you kiss me all over?" She asked as she crawled onto the bed and spread in front of the young man. After pulling a finger from her mouth and sliding it down her body, Hans can no longer control himself and quickly removed his clothing. Mounting the bed on his hands and knees, he gently connected his tongue with her luscious flower. After a few long moments of this, she'd had enough and pulled his head up so his lips met hers. Once she had cleaned herself off of his lips, she grabbed his dick and guided it into her with absolutely no effort. She felt amazing and Hans wasn't going to last very long but he tried with all his might. Adel leaned her head forward and whispered in his ear "Come on and finish already. I know you want to." Any hope he'd had was shot and he filled her up with love. His body collapses on hers and she wraps her limbs around him. Both were where each needed to be at this moment in time. He rolls off of her and lay on his back next to her. She snuggles in tight and asked, "So who are you really?" The question shot a million ideas into his head. "What do you mean?" He replied. "I can see right through you. You're in hiding." He sat up opposite of her, looking into her eyes. "Are you going to say anything to Aron?" The panic in his voice is noticeable. "I didn't plan on it. You don't scare me, I just don't believe your story." A slight smirk graced her lips. "He was ready to shoot us when we arrived! You're sure you'll keep our secret?" She giggled before kissing his lips. "You have no need to worry about little old me." Relieved, he kept it frank. "We're on our way out of Europe to Argentina. We're no longer safe here." She caressed his face with her hand and snuck another kiss. "Your secret is safe with me. Thank you for not lying to me." The pair got comfortable together and Hans slept in the bed with her that night. He enjoyed another couple of encounters before sneaking back to his room in the early morning hours to avoid detection.

The rooster's greeting at daybreak seemed to come just as he closed his eyes. The thought of hacking off its head creeped into his mind. Before these thoughts took root, a light smack to the face made him open his eyes. Josef was sitting up, smiling at him. "Get up lover boy. We need to eat and get on the road." With an extended groan, Hans sat himself up. "Let's get this over with." As they gather their belongings, Aron stomps into the room. "Wrap these blankets up for your journey. You've got a lot of distance to go between here and Budapest. Doubtful you'll find someone as nice as me to house you." His deep belly laugh filled the house. "Adel is up early making big breakfast. Come, come." With this, he leaves the room. Hans cocks a smile and says "She did. More than once." Josef swings his open hand toward the young man's head, but he narrowly dodged it at the last second. "I'm sorry! I'm sorry!" He laughed as he talked. "I'm feeling really good. Tired, but good." A smirk graces Josef's lips. "Just keep your mouth shut until we're on the road." He gives a silent acknowledgment, and the provisions are packed tightly into their backpacks before they ventured out to the main room for breakfast.

Adel moved about the room preparing something that smelled heavenly. Hans mentally noted her beautiful glow this morning. She was alone in the room, but the sound of giggling children and Aron yelling was present elsewhere in the house. Their eyes locked as she noticed them entering the room. "Quickly, come here you two!" She whispered, loud enough for only them to hear. Hans dropped his bag near Josef's and followed him over. "I just wanted to let you guys know I took care of your little sacks." A moment passed before the panic set in. Their faces must've given it away because she started to laugh. "No one will ever find them or know what was in them.

Relax. Come sit and enjoy the food I'm making! This is a special meal." Josef's face still showed some doubt though he sat upon the bench without a word. Hans did the same, awaiting the last good meal he'd have for a couple of weeks.

The yelling and laughing began to get louder until the source stampeded into the room. Aron and the three children were full of energy and gathered around the fire, near the men. "Oh wow!" Aron screams as he sits. "We haven't had cabbage rolls since" he thinks hard for a moment. "I don't even remember when. You must've made quite an impression on young Adel!" With a giggle she says, "Well I had fresh meat to use and we don't often have guests." The belly laugh filled the room. Hans wasn't sure whether he'd miss it or not but he was still in no position to complain. This whole ordeal had turned out much better than he ever thought it would. "No complaints from me here!" Aron adds. "Well I'm starving." Hans said. "Worked up an appetite sleeping last night." The smile on Adel's lips also grew on Hans'. Josef sighed with relief that Aron was too busy tending to the children to notIce. "Food is ready everyone!" Adel announced as she began to dish out portions. Breakfast is filled with Aron's crazy stories, the children laughing, and loving glances between Hans and Adel. Once they had eaten their fill, the men stood to leave. "You have been most gracious. All of you." Josef announced to the room. "Yes, thank you!" Hans throws in. "Always happy to help nice travelers. Especially in this time. Nice people are hard to come by. It was our pleasure." The way Aron said this was remarkably different than his normal brute tone. "Hans!" Adel said as she stood from her seat. "I've got something else for your journey. Come here quickly!" She began walking toward the room they had slept, waving her arm for him to follow.

As he was about to enter the door, her arms reached out and grabbed him. He tripped into her arms and she kissed him. "Thank you for everything." She whispers to him. "You've brought some excitement into my dreary life." He gently kissed her forehead. "You've certainly made my stay a pleasure. I should be thanking you. Could I write you?" He asked. Her smile reached from ear to ear. "I would love to keep in contact with you." She stepped away to a nearby table and wrote her address on a piece of paper. "Write me once you arrive in Argentina safely." She said to him as she handed him the note. He placed the paper in his wallet. "Take these gloves and get going. You've got a long journey ahead!" She handed him two pairs of homemade fleece mittens and walked with him toward the doorway. "Kiss me again?" She asked. Not wishing to disappoint, Hans showered her with kisses before stepping back out into the main room. Josef was already packed up and waiting near the exit. "Have a safe trip friends!" Aron said as he waved. The children follow suit. A wave back and a wink to Adel saw the men out the door, back into the cold. Hans gave Josef his set of gloves. "A parting gift from my dear beloved." He smiled as he put his hand into his glove. "Warm" Josef shared. "Should make the trek more bearable. Sun's out too." He pointed to the sky. Hans took a deep breath while stretching his back. He audibly let the air out of his lungs. "Let's get to it" he says before beginning down the path and up the road into the unknown.

The night of rest they had and the home cooked food had already made this leg of the trip more enjoyable. Not a soul had bothered the men up to this point and it had been a couple of days since they departed Aron's. They'd passed a few groups of farmers and even a Red Army patrol had driven right by. No one had batted an eye. "I don't think we'd have made it this far without finding that house. We look like locals." Hans said. Josef nods in agreement. "I'm very thankful for the clothing. It's warm and we do blend in well. Don't foresee any issues." Shadows began to shift as the sun started to set. The winter had been rough this year but Aron and Adel had brought some normalcy to the odd turn of events they were calling life. Another night would pass under the stars but the provisions given to them made it bearable. Hans thought of Adel before he slept, as he had every night since they met. He longed for a time when he might meet her again.

The main road they travelled along took them through a village on the outskirts of the city. Hans could see the building tops of Budapest on the horizon so he knew they were approaching their destination. Icicles hung from the window sills, casting rainbows across the cobblestone streets. "Beautiful" Hans thought, but quaint compared to the Europe he was used to. "Budaors?" Josef said pointing to a sign. "Almost there by Aron's list." "Aron's list?" Hans asked. "Yea. Look." Josef handed him a piece of paper. A list of names was written on it. "These are the towns we should pass through to easily find ourselves in Budapest. Budaors is the last town on the list." "Aron was a great guy" Hans thought to himself. This trip began doomed to fail but here they were, almost to the end. The kindness of strangers was shocking, even in a time filled with so much dread. "Nearly there. Let's make haste to avoid another night outside." Josef said.

It wasn't long until they came upon the Danube River and the road which brought them onto the northern tip of the island. "This is the island Herr Hitler told me about. We're to go south and we'll find the hide-out." Josef whispered. They trekked down through the paths amongst families ice skating and building snowmen with their children. A group of these children were throwing snowballs at each other. Hans laughed as one of the snowballs whizzed past Josef's head. The children shrieked and ran off. Hans followed them with his eyes as they ran, taking in the scenery. Josef had the last laugh though as the next snowball thrown hit Hans square in the face. "I guess I asked for that" Hans laughed. "Watch your back old man" Hans jests. They share a laugh and continue travelling south.

Once past the populated area, the ruins of an ancient monastery come into view, just as the directions had described. "We're looking for a Sundial." Josef explained, wracking his brain to remember everything he was told. "We're to push the dial in?" He said, questioning his memory. After a moment, happy with his recall, he told Hans "Apparently that's it." They split up to search around what looked to have once been a garden. Hans' initial search appeared to be fruitless as he found nothing resembling a sundial. He trudged back towards Josef across the courtyard. Midway through, his foot snagged on a something causing him to fall face first into the snow. He lay there for a moment, laughing at himself. The crunching of Josef's feet was getting louder. Hans looked up to see him running toward where he lay. After determining he was ok and having a laugh at his expense, Josef helped him sit up. As Hans looked back at what he tripped on, a glimmer of something blinked up at him. It appeared that tripping unburied something from under the snow. He scrambled to his knees, furiously digging. "Josef, look! I've found something." Josef quickly kneeled by his side, helping him uncover the tarnished copper Sundial. Hans glanced over his shoulder, scanning the area, making sure no one was around. Satisfied that the coast was clear he nodded and Josef pushed the dial.

Nothing happened. They stared at the sundial and each other. Josef checked, perhaps he hadn't pushed it hard enough? He went to press it again as a loud grinding noise became audible and the ground began to rumble beneath their feet. They scrambled backward as a nearby stone wall split down the middle, scrapping apart, revealing a small opening. As the rumbling ceased, a set of moss covered steps were revealed, leading down. The men glanced at each other, shrugged, and cautiously started down the stairs. Just as Hans cleared his head, the door slowly groaned back to its closed position. They had no lights and were soon in complete darkness. Hans laughs "Well this is great". As if he was heard by someone, or something, lights burst on inside the cave.

This was no mere hole in the ground they had entered. It felt much like the offices in the capital building back in Berlin. Polished hardwood frames were hanging on delicate plaster walls and were filled with paintings. A large mahogany desk with a fancy electric light complete with jeweled inlays sat in the middle of the room. The feel of the room reminded Hans of the Fuhrer's office. He'd been there recently enough to remember and decided this was a smaller replica of that room. Josef was closely inspecting one of the paintings. "The decorations are real." he noted in awe. "I think this is the Fuhrer's office. Or at least a very good replica." Hans stated. "This place is heated too?" He asked. "Feels like it. I didn't know places like this existed." Josef replied. The men unbundled themselves before continuing to explore the hideout.

Beyond the office where they entered, they found a fully stocked pantry which was attached to a large industrial kitchen. Through the kitchen was a study with rows upon rows of bookcases. They continued up a spiral staircase on the far side of the study and found multiple sleeping rooms with large beds in each, eight total. At the end of this hallway was a large shower room. "Now that's a sight for sore eyes" Hans said. "It's been weeks since I've had a proper wash." Josef laughed out loud, pinched his nose, and said "You're preaching to the choir son." Hans laughed with him. "Well lucky for you, that's where I'm headed now. I'll meet you back downstairs soon." Josef nodded. "I'm more interested in cooking something than washing up right now anyway. That kitchen looks marvelous." "Oh damn, a hot shower and a hot meal? Our luck continues to grow." Hans said excitedly. "Go wash up. It'll be nearly ready by the time you're done." Josef told him before heading back toward the entrance.

Hans couldn't remember a time when he was this happy about having access to running water. It was a luxury, even in his extravagant lifestyle, and he knew going to the front, he'd be without it for a while but after everything that'd happened and his rendezvous with Adel, he was in need of a solid wash. He removed his dirty clothes and set them in a pile near the door before entering the shower room. It felt great to be naked but all the odor protection the clothes afforded him was now gone. He quickly turned the dial and his mouth dropped in awe. Water began falling from the ceiling and jets were spraying him from the sides as well. "This shower was heaven" He thought. The water never got cold so he didn't get out for a long while. Once his fingers had started to prune and he had pleasured himself more than one time, he decided it was time to eat.

Fluffy towels were stacked near the exit so Hans wrapped himself in one before he entered one of the sleeping rooms they'd passed while exploring the bunker.

The ornate setup of the room had him feeling like he had walked into the Hotel Adlon. For a brief moment, he forgot about the current situation he was in. He dropped the towel and pounced onto the big bed. He laid there for a moment, stretching and relaxing. His stomach gave a mighty growl as he laid there. "Still need to eat" he thought. Curious what he could wear that was clean, he walked over to the closet. Dress clothes hung on the bar, organized by color and size. Grabbing a pair of slacks and a nice shirt in his size, he headed over to the vanity. Hans bent over to put on a clean pair of socks when a voice startled him. "Damn boy, that's a site for sore eyes eh?" He lost his footing and fell over to tune of Josef's raucous laughter. "I wondered what was taking so long. I see know that an anaconda attacked you." He was still laughing. Hans' face was beet red. "Get dressed boy. Foods piping hot!" Josef let out another good laugh before turning around and entering the hallway. Hans could hear him laughing as he walked away. He stood and quickly dressed. "I'll get his old ass. Just wait." He chuckled to himself as he admired himself in the nice clothes he'd found. With a final glance of himself in the mirror, he slipped into his shoes and took off for the kitchen, eager to see what Josef had prepared.

Josef had been frying up something wonderful, that much was clear. The smell was permeating all the way up into the study and Hans' stomach was going crazy with hunger pains. As he entered the kitchen, he finally got to lay his eyes on the spread. He was shocked. It had smelled like a five course meal at Reinstoff but turned out to just be Spam and beans. He surmised that eating field rations for long enough could make any home cooked meal seem gourmet. "It's not much but it smells wonderful doesn't it?" Josef asked when he realized Hans had come in. "It does smell good and I'm feeling ravenous." Hans answered while grabbing a dish. "We should've brought Adel with us. Those cabbage rolls? That stew?" Hans trailed off. "I knew you were real sweet on her." Josef smiles. "Be thankful she is safe though." His face turned serious. "At this point, the Allied Nations will be hunting for us and our German brothers for war crimes. I have no idea what Herr Hitler's plan is moving forward but just be thankful the ones you care about are not here with us." He nodded as he took his first bite. Josef's word were full of truth but it didn't quench his longing for her. "That is true. Have you any idea what might be happening? What we're going to be asked to do?" Once he had swallowed the food in his mouth, Josef replied "I don't but I'm slightly worried about the whole affair. This whole situation seems fishy. Shouldn't worry until we know though. Enjoy the time we have here. We're safe for now." Agreeing, Hans silently finished his dinner.

Over the next couple of weeks, Hans and Josef spent their time as relaxed as possible. Hans had scoured the library multiple times, finding books he was interested in reading. A stack of tomes was beginning to pile up next to his bed. Josef had dug deep into the pantry stores and cooked all day long. The men ate like war time royalty. Not knowing what trials and tribulations lay ahead, the men used the down time to recharge, physically and mentally. Many relaxing days passed and Hans was warm, comfortable, and content. Josef's experience had been much of the same. Little did Hans know tonight would be the last night of this extended period away from the horrors of the world.

Josef was buried deep in a cupboard, as he had been the majority of their stay in the bunker, digging for breakfast ingredients when the floor began to gently vibrate. He popped his head out and saw that Hans had joined him the kitchen. "What's that?" Hans asked. "The door?" Josef stood and walked out of the kitchen, down to the office where the entrance was located. A group of eight men came down the steps dressed in mostly black and grey. Nothing significant to note about the men other than they were German as one was speaking it. Hans looked for Herr Hitler but did not see the moustache. One of the group proceeded forward and shrugged off his coat. He draped it over the back of a chair. The man approached Josef with an extended hand. "Josef Dietrich and Hans Lorenz I presume?" He asked in English. Josef answered "Yes, that's us" as he shook the man's hand. He proceeded to ask Josef about their trip. Hans watched the interaction and the man's mannerisms as he spoke but couldn't place them. He knew this man. The smirk that graced his face while speaking and the way he flipped his hair out of his eyes were oddly familiar. It finally hit Hans as he continued to watch Josef and the man converse. Hans came to attention as the truth clicked in his mind. He threw his right arm out and screamed "Seig heil". Josef followed suit where he was standing. The man quickly stepped over to Hans while shaking his head and lowered his arm. "Friends." The man started "We have much to discuss but do not salute anyone in this fashion. Ever again. It's for all of our safety." Hans and Josef relax and continue to listen. "The Third Reich is done and I am no longer in charge. Of anything. I'd like to see us as equals in coming times." Josef's disbelief was written all over his face "But Herr

Hitler?" he managed. "Call me Adam, if you please, Josef. I'll be the most wanted man in the world soon if not already. The name Adolf Hitler needs to rest." Hans had never seen Josef's emotions look so uncontrolled. "Allow the rest of the party to get comfortable. We've had a long journey. We will meet soon, now that we have all arrived, and I'll attempt to explain the situation."

With that, the group shuffled upstairs leaving Josef and Hans alone in the office. Josef still hadn't fully processed what was happening. "Let's continue breakfast. I'm still starving." Hans suggests. Josef looked at him with pure defeat written on his face. "I'm sure they will explain what's happened. Don't worry about it right now." Hans told him. The men returned to the kitchen and made a breakfast big enough to share with everyone who had just arrived. The smell rose through the bunker and the new arrivals found their way down to the kitchen, a couple at a time. Hans noticed that while cooking, Josef seemed to be taking this better. He interacted normally with the men as he served them breakfast. Hans shrugged it off and with a full belly, went to the study to find a book to bury his face in. Josef stayed in the kitchen and cleaned up from breakfast. His solace had been in the kitchen. He worried about all of this. He'd been affiliated with the party since before it was named the Nazi party. Hitler, the Fuhrer, was a mere man at this point. There was no more Reich, no more structure. The party was finished. He worked through his uncertainty in the kitchen and kept it inside as best he could. He'd keep it under wraps until the group had the meeting and he had all the facts.

Once he'd finished in the kitchen, Josef found his way up to the shower. He was cordial with the men but avoided conversation as he passed. A warm shower would be just what he needed to help decompress. The shower was empty so Josef didn't waste any time and got in. He found this shower magical. The room was large and the warm water came from all directions, never getting cold. He began to wash himself and was startled as he turned around. One of the new arrivals was in the shower room with him. "Not odd in itself" He thought because the room was built to house more than one body but the man's dick was hard. That struck Josef as odd. "Guten Tag" he said to the man and continued his wash. "Guten tag" the man responded. He watched the man out of the corner of his eye. He hugged the wall and moved to a far corner of the shower. His eyes were on Josef the whole time and when he reached the corner, he took his cock in his hand and began stroking it. Not having the energy to deal with this, he finished rinsing and got out, not looking at or saying another word to the man. He grabbed a towel and went to the room he'd been staying in to get some fresh clothes. Once dressed, he set out to find Hans.

Out of the eight that had entered, Josef noted that half were nothing more than bodyguards. He guessed as much because they were standing at attention in key vantage points away from the rest and were not speaking as the others were, if at all. Entering the study, he noticed the man from the shower sitting next to Hans, who had his face buried in a book as usual. The other two men were standing near the top of the staircase speaking. The Shorter of the two made eye contact with Josef as he entered the room. "Josef, are you refreshed and ready to begin?" he asked. Josef looked at the man, trying to remember where he'd seen his face before. "Adolf Eichmann" the man answered as if reading Josef's mind. "Lieutenant colonel in charge of logistics?" Josef asked. "In another life." He smiled.

"This is Albert Kesselring." He pointed to the other man. "You may have heard of him as well." He continued. "Of course I have. The Reich General the rest of us aspired to be" Josef remembered fondly. "I appreciate that" Albert replied with a smile. "Unfortunately, no longer. Just a civilian part of this collective."

Eichmann interjected "Herr Hitler, err Adam, was waiting for us to reconvene. I'll let him know we're ready." He stepped past Josef and proceeded down the hall towards the bed chambers. "It's a pleasure to be in your company Albert" Josef said as he extended his hand for a shake. "The pleasure is mine." Albert replied. "You've a very impressive record yourself." "I'll be looking forward to exchanging war stories but please excuse me while I check in with my man Hans" Josef ended the conversation and started down the staircase. "Wow" he thought. This was turning into quite the day. He wondered if Hans knew who these men were. His curiosity had reached a new level. "What were they going to learn?" He asked himself.

Hans had found a new book on the mystery of the Thule society during his search of the tomes along the wall. With this book, he found a comfortable chair and dug in. After a few minutes of reading, he heard some men talking in the hall and it sounded as if they were headed toward the study. He wasn't bothered by this and kept reading about the secret bases, the hidden islands, and all the wonder of this ancient society. One of the men went to a case and also grabbed a book. He stalked over and sat near Hans. The man was staring at him so Hans put down his book to initiate the inevitable interaction. "Josef. Josef Mengele." The man said. His name rang a bell. "The doctor?" Hans asked. "Quite so. Quite so." He replied. Hans got a very odd feeling from the man but kept polite. "It's a pleasure to make your acquaintance" Hans said. He attempted to end the conversation by telling the doctor "We can speak later if you please, I've just gotten to some very gripping material." The man replied "That would be wonderful. You've got intriguing features." Hans hid his face in his book and took a moment to shake off the uneasy feeling that plagued him before continuing.

Moments later, Adam walked back into the study, followed by Eichmann, and proclaimed "Great! Everyone is here." He rubbed his hands together as he spoke. "Let's gather and get comfortable. I have much to tell you". All the standing men shuffled toward the center of the study. Josef found his way into a seat next to Hans. Adam was the last to come down the staircase and planted himself on a leather chair in the center of the group. "Friends" He begins. "What I'm about to tell you is going to defy what you know to be reality." Everyone's attention was drawn in. "I'm going to come right out with it." He continued. "The man you see before you now, is not the man who organized the conquest of Europe. I am not the man who ordered the slaughter of millions of people." The group was very confused and eyes were darting around to one another, gauging the reactions of one another. "I have been possessed for much of my adult life. I remember every situation I've been a part of but I was not in the driver's seat for any portion of it." "Possessed?" Kesselring belts out. "By what?' he adds, skeptical in tone. Adam sighs. "I'm not able to answer that question because I do not know. Whatever it was, it wanted blood; chaos. Look at what we've done to the world." After this statement, you could see the tears welling up in his eyes. "I do not blame any of you for what you've done." He held back his emotions as he continued. "Whatever it was that possessed me, knew of a way to command people to do its bidding. What is important now is that you know where I really stand and you know the truth."

An air of unbelief hung about the room. You could almost hear the gears turning in the men's head as they attempted to process what was just told to them. Hans whispered to Josef "This took a big turn from where I thought it was going." Josef nodded his agreeance but was unable to form words at the moment. The doctor spoke up next. "Herr Adam, how was it you came to be free from this possession?" "Please, friends." Adam begins "We must forget our previous lives and titles. We should all be thinking of new aliases. Adam, will do just fine. That is a good question though." He was thoughtful for a moment. "The first time I remember being in control of myself was in the bunker back in Berlin. Allied planes were bombing the capital and people were frantic. My possessed body was planning to escape but the SS Captain did not think we would be able to get away safely. He suggested suicide as an alternative to getting captured by the Allied Forces." Adam took a moment to pause.

Everyone in the room was deeply engaged in the story and eagerly awaiting him to continue. "Once the men locked Eva and me in our room" a tear streamed down his cheek as he spoke, "I watched as Eva took the cyanide given to her. I'd never wanted to be in control more than that moment. As she began to struggle breathing, I regained control of my body and was able to hold her as she passed. I've no idea the reason or the means but I've been in full control since that moment." The room was completely silent.

"That sounds like a story out of a fable book." Eichmann's statement broke the silence. The room was skeptical with him. "Had I heard this from another person, I wouldn't have believed it either." Adam said. Hans stood to ask "How did you escape the room? You said you were locked in?" A couple of men audibly agreed with the question. "Coming back in control was only the beginning of an odd set of events." Adam stood. "The building rumbled hard like a bomb had landed on top of us. A far wall split apart." He was waving his hands around as he talked. "An opening formed and it was just big enough for me to squeeze through. I crawled into the hole which dropped me into the sewers beneath the city." Now standing and having answered the questions presented, Adam delivered his pitch. "Come with me to Argentina." He pleaded. "We have a powerful new ally who can explain the situation better. He appeared to me out of the shadows while I was in the sewers. I believe he can equip us with the necessary tools to survive this. He will have answers for us. I know it." Silence filled the room once more.

Kesselring bellowed out "Well, we're all dead men here in Europe anyhow. I'm in." Eichmann stands and throws in "He's got a good point. We've followed you here, why not to safety in South America? I'm in." Mengele stood but remained silent. Hans looked to Josef and their eyes met. The confusion in each other was obvious. Josef stood but had words. "Herr Hit...Adam, the majority of my life has been in the Third Reich and your final solution for the world. Now, you expect me to just abandon all of this and take a holiday?" The room looked at him, visibly stunned by his comment but not in disagreement. Adam's face is devoid of emotion and Hans is worried they're about to witness one of his famous outbursts. Much to everyone's surprise, he very calmly replies "No. That's not what I want at all."

The room perked up awaiting further explanation. "The men who served me and Germany were under as much a spell as I was." He began with. "Look inside yourself Josef and tell me the work we were doing was what you wanted. Tell me it's what you desired." Josef sits down, placing his face in his hands. "Well, no. It's not what I'd hoped to be doing as a boy." He finally is able to say. "We've been doing the errand of a fiend." Adam tells the men. "I'm done with that and I'm ready to try to destroy the evil we've been working for. Are you men with me?" The remainder of the men stood in agreeance. Josef sat for a moment longer, though he did also stand after a short period. "This entire thing is wild but I'm willing to continue following you" Josef added. The joy was obvious on Adam's face. "Friends," He says, "I'm honored to be here with your support. As I find out more details about this event, you will learn them with me. Let us help cleanse the world of the filth we've brought to it." To that, the men cheered. "We leave for South America in the morning. We will be safe there to plan our counter." "What is our plan Adam?" Eichmann asked. "To rid the world of the evil that possessed us; by any means necessary."

1: IN THE HOME OF HIS PARENTS

"Monday morning again" Ronan thought as he lay in bed. His phone started blaring the alarm he set the night before. Ronan felt around under the pillows looking for the phone to shut it up. Once he found the snooze button, he stayed in bed for another few minutes enjoying the silence. A lot of loud banging sounds from the kitchen disrupted his solace. "Food!" It took a second to process the thought but once it hit him, he sat up quickly. He twisted his back and got in a good stretch to help wake his body before finally jumping out of the bed. "The fuck are my slippers?" he thought as he scanned his floor. "Oh, there they are" he whispered to himself as he wiggled his toes into the fluffy shoes. Lastly, he snagged a towel that was draped over the back of his computer chair and took off for the shower.

Ronan was in need of some help waking up today and this shower just wasn't doing it. He stood, unmoving, as the water streamed onto his face and down his body, all the while wanting to go back to sleep. Not getting what he needed from the shower, he finished rinsing the shampoo from his head and turned off the water. It took an inordinate amount of time for him to find his way out of the bathroom. The hope of hot coffee was all that kept him moving. Once he made it back to his room, he stopped by his computer to put on some music. Avatar was up in his iTunes so he clicked on "Hail the Apocalypse" and made his way to the closet. He started to gently bob his head as he dug through the closet, looking for something to wear. Air drumming his way out of the closet, he reared his back to sing along "There's a" and proceeded to whip his hair around as the music started again.

Finally feeling refreshed, Ronan finished dressing for the day before heading downstairs to see what mom was making for breakfast. He snuck from the bottom of the stairs toward the swinging doors which led to the kitchen. Once he reached the end of the hall, he stepped through the doors quickly and screamed "EMMA!" attempting to make her jump. "I heard you coming down the stairs" She says, clearly un-phased by him at this point in their life together. She continued with preparing food without skipping a beat. "What was it?" She asked. "You walk so loud, I could have shot you in the dark?" she chuckles. "Breathes, mum. Breathes." He shakes his head and chuckles with her.

Emma Corvers was 5'2" on a good day. They made a pair as Ronan stood well over 6'. She was the sweetest person in the world. Emma volunteered all over town when she wasn't at home, keeping up the house for Ronan and his dad. Henrik Corvers was a special agent at the local F.B.I. office. Dad wasn't home much so Ronan spent most of his time with Mom. Overall, Ronan was a happy kid with a good life. The couple had adopted him when he was an infant. Ronan knew nothing about his birth parents and they never talked about the subject. Ronan never really worried about it. As far as he was concerned, the Corvers were his parents.

"Thanks for breakfast ma" he says after he kisses her on the cheek. "Remember" She starts "you're supposed to go meet that nice older couple after school today." Ronan smiles. "I didn't forget! Taylor's coming over with me." He replies. "You never know; they could be serial killers!" he says as his smile turns into his signature 'smartass' smirk. "Get out of here before you're late for school" Emma replies, ignoring his sarcasm but smirking herself. "Oh!" She says. "Don't be out too

late, your uncle Mason is coming over for dinner tonight."
Ronan's face lights up. "Oh nice! I'll be home for that. I haven't
seen him for a while!" Emma smiles. "Great. I'm sure he'll be
happy to see you too." He hugs her again. "I'll see you later
mum, I'm out! Love you!" He says as he spins around and heads
for the door. "Love you" she calls back behind him.

He hit the street running and headed up to the corner
of Harvard Terrace and Harvard Ave. It was where he usually
met Taylor in the morning. She wasn't there yet but he peaked
around the building and saw her coming. He thought she was
the most beautiful thing. Taylor was 5'3" with a wonderfully
thick booty. Her pale white skin was dotted with tattoos and
currently had a mild sunburn. She had her bright blue hair up in
two space buns this morning, one of his favorites. Ronan
couldn't help but focus on her breasts bouncing as she walked
toward him. They had been friends since he could remember
though they had never dated. Every day with her made this fact
harder and harder to forget. They'd talked about it years ago,
openly as they did everything, and at the time, agreed that it
didn't feel like a good decision. He thought it was different now
but was nervous to bring it up. He ducked back behind the wall
to try and startle her. He was still salty that his first attempt this
morning failed miserably.

"Hey you goof, I can see you" she giggles. He walks out
from around the corner, defeated. "Dang, I tried scaring mom
today too and all I got was some half assed attempt at a Lord of
the Rings quote." She laughed out loud. "I love you two" she
says. "Well we love you" he smiles at her. They fall in step with
each other while walking toward the subway, or T station as we
call it around here, which they took to school. "How was your
night?" Ronan asks, knowing the answer. "It's St. Mary's." She

says. "Someone's crying, someone's yelling, and no one cares that the group home attendants make room visits." The thought gives her a chill. Ronan reminds her "You know the 'rents said you're welcome to stay with us in the guest room." Knowing she was in a bad space hurt him. "I'd hate to impose. They do so much for me already." She replies. "Nope!" He says loudly. "It's decided. After we go meet the Reis' today, you're coming with me to dinner and we're gonna get you set up in the spare room." He stops walking and moves to face her. He gently grabs her shoulders and tells her "You're family Taylor. The situation there is more stressful for you than it is beneficial. It's safe and clean at my house and you're always welcome." She notices how full of compassion his eyes are and she can feel he's telling her the truth. "Ok, ok. But we need to run by and get my stuff." She agrees. "That shouldn't be a big deal." He says before smiling at her. Taylor leans forward and kisses him on the lips before beginning to walk again. Ronan stands for a moment, in shock, before picking up behind her. They both entered the station with grins on their faces.

School was just as boring as always for Ronan. His mind was elsewhere, as it usually was. Book learning about subjects he cared nothing about wasn't his idea of fun. He didn't have any classes with Taylor this semester either but he was able to see her at lunch which was nice. All the guys gave him crap for being so close to such a hot girl and not dating her. "I'll find a girl" He'd tell them. "You're all just jealous we're always together and she wants nothing to do with any of you." They'd all laugh when he told them that and usually drop it. None of them really understood anyway. They were just normal teenage boys looking to bang anything that moved, he got that. He felt that need sometimes. He brushed it all off as he always did and kept about his day as normal.

The school's lunch was terrible so the kids would usually dip out to get something from Big Tony's down the street. Tony had a little food truck he set up a couple blocks from the school every day at around the same time. He was a friendly guy and the food was amazing so they found their way down there on most days. "Kids!" Tony yells as they walk up. "I've got something I need to run by you two…" He trailed off as he turned and began digging through some boxes. "What is it Tony?" Taylor asks him. He popped back up holding a clear bag filled with something yellow. "Got some new cheese for the steak. Supplier gave me a bag to try. I wanna know what you guys think before I start selling it!" He seemed excited. "Whip us up a couple cheese steaks!" Ronan ordered, chuckling. "Aw yea, I knew you kids would help me out". Ronan looks to Taylor and they giggle to each other as the man drops some shaved steak onto the grill. Taylor began to tell Ronan about the previous night while they waited for the food to cook. After a few moments of listening to the horror she faced daily, Tony's boisterous voice called out "Come get it!" The kids walk back up to the truck and graciously accept the sandwiches. "On the house." Tony tells them. "I need to know if I should sell this" He reminds them. The kids thank him for the food. "We'll let you know! See you soon. Thanks again." Ronan says to him before leaving the cart.

He walks with Taylor to a shaded spot under a nearby tree. "Let's sit here" She suggests. Ronan loved these relaxing lunches with her. He looked forward to two things during the day; lunch with Taylor and leaving school to do things with her. The stories she told him about the group home made his blood boil. He knew Mom and Dad wouldn't mind helping and he was so happy he was able to do something to help her. "Tay" He says. "Ro." She replies playfully. "I'm so thankful you're a part of my life." He tells her. "You just get me. It's so easy to be me around you." She giggles and tells him "I've never had the chance to do anything for you. I've never been in the place to do so. Thank you for everything you and your parents do for me." She leans in for a kiss and softly places her lips on his. Slowly pulling away, she holds her face close to his. They lock eyes and Ronan asks her "So what are these? And why are they happening?" Her lip curls into a devious smile. "I can stop if that's what you want?" He rushes in to steal another kiss from her. "That's not what I said" He chuckles as he pulls away. Kissing him again, she says "Well these are kisses and I want to give them to you right now, so deal with it." Taylor gets to her knees and straddles Ronan's lap while continuing to kiss him. Her stomach growls a few moments later and she starts to giggle. "Let's eat" Ronan says laughing.

Once they'd finished the sandwiches, the kids ran back to Tony's and let him know what they thought. "I loved it!" Taylor told him. "Very ok by me" Ronan added. Tony's face lit up. "I knew I could count on you kids! Goes into the sandwiches tomorrow!" They thanked him one last time before making their way back toward the school. Ronan stops once the school comes into view and exhales loudly. Taylor smiles and kisses him. "Let's get back and get it over with" She tells him. "Fineeeeeee" He replies through a smile. They kiss one more time before separating and going to their next blocks.

The school day dragged after lunch. Ronan's mind was occupied with the events to come and math was the last thing on his mind this afternoon. The teacher was explaining some asinine concept with letters and numbers and he was completely tuned out. It seemed like both a flash and an eternity before the last bell finally rang, freeing him from this hell. Once it finally went off, Ronan was up and in the hallway before it had even finished. He was nearly to the place he usually met Taylor, the entrance to the library, when a small object quickly moved into his way, stopping his movement. "Hi Ronan" the little girl says. Trying not to show his annoyance, he replies "Oh hi Lisa, I'm actually…" She interrupts his sentence "When are you going to take me out on a date?" She asks. "Maybe sometime but I am very busy today." He looks up and can see Taylor belly laughing at the scene she's been watching. "So we'll talk later ok?" Before she can reply, he slips around her and begins moving quickly toward his destination. "I'm going to hold you to that!" Lisa yells after him. "Let's do this" He says as he walks up next to Taylor, admiring her ass as he usually did. They exit the door together and continue moving quickly to make sure no stragglers follow. They slow the pace as they round a corner and the school is out of sight. The walk is quiet for a moment while Ronan internally reflects on how annoying Lisa is. Taylor breaks the silence "So you gonna tap that?" He leers at her to see if she's smiling. "She's got some great boobs and even has a tattoo on one of them! I bet she's a freak." She says, completely straight faced. Knowing she's being a shithead, he gives her the stink eye causing her to break out in laughter. Her laugh is infectious so he joins her. "Man I wish she'd take a hint" He says. "Knowing girls are throwing themselves at you is actually kind of hot. Makes me want you more." She runs her hand over his dick as she says this. Ronan puts his arm around the small of her back while cupping one of her breasts with his other. "Ms. Quinn, save that for later" He whispers to her before he kisses her. The blush sets in on her cheeks. They separate and continue toward the T station, holding hands. "Mason is coming over for dinner tonight!" He excitedly tells her as they walk. "The guy who builds all the weird things right?" She asks while giggling. He opens the station door and holds it for her. "Yea! Him!" He answers. "He's nice" She remembers aloud. "I've always liked him."

The older couple only lived a few blocks from school and but Ronan really liked being underground so he took the T as often as possible. "What did mom tell you about this couple?" Taylor asked while they rode. Mom had always found things for him to do around town to help people out. He didn't mind and in exchange, his parents took care of his bills like his cell phone and Xbox live. The Reis' needed some help with cleaning and such around the house. "Just that they were Jewish immigrants who moved here after WWII. They don't have any kids and they are getting too old to keep up the house by themselves." Ronan answered. "They used to own a pawn shop so I bet they have a lot of cool stuff." He added, clearly interested in that tidbit. "Cool. I hope they're nice!" Taylor says. "Mom told me they are. She's a good judge of character so I trust her." Ronan tells her as the train enters their stop.

After climbing a few flights of stairs, they were back out on the busy street. The couple's brownstone was only a block or so over from here on Pearl. Once they got onto Pearl Street, he grabbed mom's note to check what number the house was. "336" He says aloud. He was trying to acclimate himself to decide where they needed to walk but Taylor was already moving. "Come on silly, it's this way." She giggles. Had he been with anyone else, he'd have been super embarrassed but she was city smart so he went with it. Ronan noticed a little old lady outside of one of the houses, banging the dust out of a rug on the railing. He was following the numbers and realized she was at the house they were looking for. The kids approached and he started a conversation. "Hello ma'am. My name is Ronan Corvers and this is my friend Taylor. We're looking for the Reis residence." The old lady looked at him with a smirk. "Ma'am? What do I look like, an old lady?" She laughed out loud after asking this and the kids joined. "My name is Carma Reis. With a C." She points out. "My husband Sabra is inside making a snack. I'd say you've found us young mister Corvers and friend!" She says with a smile. "Come in, come in" Carma invites as she opens the front door and enters the house. "She seems like a funny old lady" Ronan whispers to Taylor. She smiles and nods in agreement. The kids followed Carma inside the house.

"Have a seat on the couch" Carma points to the living room on her way into the kitchen. The house looked like any other old person's he'd ever been into. He was slightly disappointed that he didn't see any cool pawn shop items laying around. Taylor had already sat down and was trying to get his attention as he peaked around the house. They hear Carma scream her husband's name and giggle. "Sabra, the kids are here!" She yells. "Move your tuckus!" She comes back into the room and drops onto a couch opposite them. Carma looks at Ronan, then shifts her attention to Taylor. "Are you two dating?" she asks. "I'm nosey" she adds. Ronan says "We've been friends since we were toddlers and we've talked about it but funny you should ask Mrs. Reis, I think I'll have an answer for you next time we meet". She looks at him cross. "You know my name boy! Use it" She cackles and points to Taylor. "I ask because I see *her* and how she looks at you." Ronan looks over at Taylor and had never seen her cheeks so red. Before anyone can continue the conversation, there's a bang in the hallway that calls everyone's attention; much to Taylor's relief.

A tall man with a solid head of white hair comes around the corner with a tray stacked high with treats. "Oh boy!" he proclaims. "It's been ages since I made something for someone who actually wanted to eat it." He looks at his wife and sticks his tongue out. Taylor laughs. "You two crack me up" she says. "Well aren't you a pretty one!" He places the tray on the coffee table and fixed his glasses to get a better look at her. "You best be dating this one young man" he says pointing at Ronan. Luckily, Carma saves Ronan from having to answer. "They're best friends. Like you and I were growing up in Oswiecim, leave them be to eat your dang snacks" Everyone chuckles. Sabra plops on the couch next to Carma and wears a false face of defeat. His face quickly changes to a smile and he gently kisses Carma's cheek.

"Well you've found the place." Carma says aloud. "You've met my crazy husband." She points to him and the kids giggle. Sabra smiles. "Go enjoy the evening together. I'll tell your mother you were here for a while and very helpful." She winks at them. "It was a pleasure to meet you." Ronan says as he stands. "The pleasure was all ours." Sabra replies. "We'll see you two soon. Have fun tonight!" He adds. "Thank you" The kids reply in unison. Taylor grabs another treat after she stood and exchanges a smile with Sabra on their way out. "I like them" she says. "Yea, they're pretty funny." Ronan chuckles. "I think we're going to have some fun helping them out. Now let's go grab your stuff. I'll be happier with you out of that place." Taylor flashes him a smile behind his back like Cupid's arrow had just struck home.

2: YEARS OF SUFFERING IN OSWIECIM

Over the next couple of months, Ronan and Taylor visited the Reis' often. The house was starting to look real organized and tidy. Sabra told the kids many fantastic stories about their lives since coming to the US though Ronan noticed he never spoke of the time before. Knowing they were Jewish, he thought it better to leave it alone because he knew what they had lived through. The kids enjoyed the Reis' company as much as the older couple was enjoying their company and assistance. Taylor was feeling very full of love, having moved into the spare bedroom at the Corver's and also spending lots of time with the nice old couple. She finally felt like she had the family she'd always dreamed of.

Once the organizing was underway, Ronan began to find the coolest stuff. Most of the pawn shop they had previously owned was stuffed in boxes down in the basement. Ronan ended up down there often, helping Sabra organize things. While moving around the boxes, Ronan kept stumbling upon items he'd never seen before. "Hey Sabra, what're these things?" Ronan called over a pile of boxes. "Oh those old things!" Sabra comments once he saw the item Ronan was holding. "They are used to hold film rolls so they don't get exposed. Those are from the 40's!" Sabra chuckles. "Wow! You've got so much cool stuff down here." Ronan says excitedly. "Well, you collect a lot of things when people sell you stuff for a living" Sabra smiles. The men continued to move the boxes around while organizing, which cleared a spot on a far wall. Ronan looked hard at the newly open wall because something seemed off. He moved closer and realized there was a large metal door, padlocked closed. "What's inside of here?" Ronan asks.

Sabra stops what he's doing and just stands there for a moment, gazing into eternity. Ronan wonders if he shouldn't have asked about the door by how Sabra was reacting. The old man sits rather abruptly on a nearby box. Ronan rushes to his side and asks "Are you alright?" Sabra replies "Once, a very long time ago. We had a son." They are both silent for what seems like forever. "We lost him during the war." He continues. Ronan feels the weight of the world on him and sits down on a nearby box. "It's hard to have anything of his laying around so we keep it all in there." Sabra pointed at the door. "Carma will go in every year on his birthday but otherwise we try to live without thinking of that time too much." He stops again. "I didn't mean to bring up any of these old memories Sabra" Ronan attempts to comfort. "Nonsense my boy" He replies with a smile. "You had no idea. It has been a very long time since we talked about him with anyone. It might be good to do just that today. Come upstairs and let's have some tea. We'll tell you about our boy." Ronan helps him stand and together they walk toward the stairs.

Taylor and Carma were sitting on the couch ruffling through some old magazines when the men came upstairs. The ladies looked over and smiled as they walked into the room. "Carma" Sabra says. His tone flagged her immediately. "What's the matter my love?" She asks, worry written on her face. "We should tell the kids about *Aleksy*." He said the name in almost a whisper. "Oh dear" she breaths out and sinks back into the couch. "What're you guys talking about?" Taylor asks, confused. "Come sit." Sabra looks over to Ronan. "We're not just a silly old couple who lives in Boston." He begins. "We're from Poland originally." Taylor moves to the couch opposite Carma offering the seat to Sabra. He shuffles over to the couch and sits next to his wife. Ronan takes a seat next to Taylor. "My father worked on the trains." Sabra began again. "And my father was the town doctor." Carma added. Sabra picks back up. "Carma and I have been friends since we were children. Young children. Our town was very small and everybody knew everybody. We were a very religious community and it was a very quiet place until men arrived one day and began to build on the west side of town, near the train station." Ronan felt Taylor shudder. They both knew where this was going. He figured she was nervous but he couldn't lie to himself; he was excited to hear the story.

"We were young teens at this time. He was my boyfriend." Carma lovingly looks at Sabra for a moment but her face turns grim again quickly. "No one knew what they were doing but his father told us to stay away from them. The smell of fear was in the air" Carma recalls. "German's were constructing buildings in our town and would not speak to us. We didn't know what had happened until prisoners began to arrive and even then, still no one had any idea what was to come." He is silent for a moment before Carma asks "Are you two certain you wish to hear this? Our tale gets very dark." Sabra nods in silent agreement. Taylor says "We're too far now to go back. I'm curious." Ronan also answers "I've done lots of research already on the topic. I have an idea of what happened but I am also very curious to hear it firsthand." "Very well then" Carma says to the room. A silent moment later, Sabra picked the story back up. "We should have seen what was coming next but the elders were all in denial." Carma adds "Denial was what caused a majority of the horrors to happen and continue happening. The men who ran our village are as much to blame

as the German's for what happened next." Sabra continues "The
German storm troopers began to ship out massive amounts of
people. My father was made to work very long hours to keep
the trains running. All of our neighbors who were not Jewish
were shipped to Gorlice to the east." Sabra stops to breathe and
reflect. Carma kisses his cheek. Ronan could feel the
anticipation growing. "Police began coming door to door,
forcing us to wear the Star of David on our clothes. It took a few
weeks yet, but they came for us too. One night. My whole
family." Sabra stops with a look on his face like he had just been
punched in the gut. Ronan gets up to go to him but he puts his
hand up. "I'm fine" He says. "It actually helps to talk about it.
The memories in my head are both beautiful and disgusting."
Ronan sits back down and puts a hand on Taylor's leg. Carma
notices Taylor blush and smile.

Sabra sits up on the edge of the couch and begins again.
"They came for us in the middle of the night. It was me, my
parents, and my younger brother. I woke up to the sounds of
screaming and crying happening out in the street. My parents
came rushing into my room and told me what was going on, but
I could only worry about what was happening to Carma and her
family. I prayed for this hell to end the entire time but God
never answered. Nothing stopped. Nothing went back to
normal. The streets were crowded with my neighbors and
friends. The noise was deafening, even from inside my house."
Taylor placed her hands into Ronan's. "We were getting
ourselves dressed when a few gunshots rang outside and that
did nothing but add to the chaos. The crowd got even louder."
Carma picked up "My family was my parents, myself, and my
two younger sisters; twins. We lived two streets over from
Sabra's family. I awoke to the screams in the street too. I went

to get my parents immediately." She stops and is silent as a tear runs down her cheek. Sabra places his hand over hers. "I walked in on German soldiers raping my mother. My father lay dead in their bed next to her, shot in the face. I was able to back out of the room before they noticed me and I ran to my sisters' beds down the hall. They were nowhere to be found. While I searched the house for my sisters, a scream rang out and then a single gunshot came immediately after. The screaming stopped. Realizing what had just happened, I ran straight out the front door, tears filling my eyes. Armed Germans were standing in front of my door and I stumbled into them. They threw me into the group of gathering Jews in the street."

Taylor started to tear up and gasped "This is horrible. I can't believe this happened so recently in history. Just doesn't seem possible." Ronan put his arm around her and hugged her close to comfort her. Sabra picked up the tale. "When my family got out to the street, my little brother was crying and would not stop despite the German's commanding us to shut him up. Fed up, one of the guards came to our steps and ripped my brother from my mother's arms." Ronan felt Taylor tense up, nervous for what came next. "They cut his pants off of him and castrated him on my front steps." Taylor began sobbing. Ronan was shocked. "He laid on my front steps, bleeding. His crying didn't stop until the other guard put a bullet through his head. The group of German's laughed as his heart stopped. I was too paralyzed by fear to react and my parents were being held at gunpoint." Sabra stopped for a moment to breath. Ronan could tell he was struggling. "He was my first loss but wouldn't be my last." He managed to get out before another moment of silence. "We were shoved into the moving crowd with the rest of the Jews." Taylor burst into tears. "It's ok child, this was a very long time ago and you must hear all about this for the tale to make sense." Carma says to comfort Taylor. Ronan hands her a tissue from the table. "So Carma has now lost her parents and sisters, I'm with my parents but I've lost my brother, and no one knows what is happening. I'd never seen chaos like this." Sabra stops to reflect.

Ronan whispers to Taylor "Are you ok?" while rubbing her back. "Yea I'll be fine. It was just never this real in history class." She whispers back to him. Sabra perks back up and continues. "So they lead us into the buildings they had been constructing on the other side of town. Some sort of work camp by the looks of it. There was a big metal sign above the gate they brought us through. I'll never forget what it said. Work. Makes. Free." Ronan interjects "Arbeit Macht Frei." Sabra looks at him with a minute smile. "Yes my boy, yes. You have done your research." Ronan's touch of pride quickly faded as the situation didn't call for it. Carma continued from here. "There were guards and doctors separating the group of people into two different lines. It seemed most of the older folks were going left toward a brick building in the distance and most the young people were going right. The brick building had a large smokestack and sat upon a hill. I was standing in a daze until I ran into Sabra which lifted my spirits!" Carma smiled, she seemed to fondly remember the emotion, but only for a moment before her frown came back. "The feeling didn't last. In the same moment I ran into them, we were thrown into the right gate as his parents were pushed left." Sabra chimes in. "That was the last time we ever saw my parents alive." Taylor nudges closer to Ronan. "We were stripped naked and made to stand in a line with the rest of the town. Men began to shave the hair from our bodies with dull blades." "Delousing." Ronan says quietly. Sabra nods in agreement and continues "They gave us striped uniforms to wear and showed us to the barracks where they expected us to sleep. All wood bunks. No blankets or padding." Carma motions to Sabra to come closer to her. "Took me a few weeks but I found where Sabra was living" She said. "I was looking for her too." Sabra adds. "It was a very big place and the trains never stopped. Full of people." Carma smiles at her husband. "We snuck to see each other every day. He was the only thing keeping me going." He notices and smiles back. "And she was all I had to look forward to in the day." After a brief moment of silence, Sabra says. "They eventually took me off stone duty and put me on a team that ran the gas operations." Responding to the look on Ronan's face, Sabra says, "You must understand, it was kill or be killed. Every day in this place brought me closer to denouncing my faith." He stops for a moment. Carma adds "I gave up god long before Sabra did. He had a hard time coming to terms with it." Sabra continues "One day, as the others before it, we came to do what we were required to do. This group of unfortunate souls had a familiar face in it though." He points to Carma. Taylor gasps. "I was pregnant you see, and my legs were beginning to swell. I was no good to put to work anymore." Ronan and Taylor perk up, anxious to hear what's about to happen. "I never knew I had it in me." Sabra starts. "The gang and I had talked about it before so as soon as I started, they followed. I signaled the man that worked the door. He locked all of us in; including our German escorts. I beat one of them to a pulp with an iron bar I had hidden behind a cabinet. The other was overrun by a few men from the group." He stood from the couch. "I wasn't about to let my baby and my girl be taken away. We'd been beaten down enough. We took their guns, we gathered the group, and we burst out of the room back into the field." Carma smiles. "I'd

never been more in love with him then I was at that moment.
He led the coup through the guards and a group of about 25 of
us escaped."

"Holy cow!" Ronan says. "You're a hero." Sabra smiles
at the compliment and sits back down next to his wife. Taylor
snuggles in tight next to Ronan. "So we did get away that day."
Sabra continues. "It took us a few hard weeks of sneaking
around after dark but we made it to Kolobrzeg, which is a
coastal town to the north. We had to dig out a few gold fillings
but we were able to charter passage on a fishing vessel to
Copenhagen. From there we traveled to Edinburgh. Nearly all of
us made it but a few were too weak. I did my best to keep as
many alive as I could." Carma rubs his back and adds "You really
did honey. You saved so many people." She picks up the tale.
"So we got to England safely and we found our way to London
which is where we met the Nokmim." Ronan perks up. "You
guys were Nazi hunters?!" He asks excitedly. "That we were my
boy" Sabra smiles. "We hunted thousands of them across the
world. It was just a giant group of survivors. It was a family. It
felt great to be surrounded by people like us and it felt even
better to be bringing these men to justice."

Ronan notices an intense look of pride on Sabra's face.
"Carma had our boy, Aleksy, in England. May 6th, 1945. It was
the happiest day of my life. I still felt like there may be a plan for
all this. A higher power giving us meaning. Giving all of our pain
purpose. Seeing his face kept some faith alive." The pain in his
voice was noticeable. "Neither of us had any family left you see,
so our brothers and sisters in the Nokmim helped us raise him."
Sabra reminisces. "You remind me of him a little." Carma says
looking at Ronan. "Very polite, helpful, and loving." She notices
Taylor blushing wildly again. "The hunt had become our life's

work." She continues the story. "So of course our son grew up to be involved. He had gotten really close to a man named Hanns who was one of the leaders." Sabra sounds proud to tell them "Aleksy became quite a fighter and I'd never seen someone shoot as well as him. He was making runs with the best of us as a young teen." His demeanor darkens. "All was well until we ran a mission looking for the Angel of Death." Ronan grits his teeth. "Mengele." He says. The old couple both nod. "We'd pushed his wife and found where he was hiding. Argentina. The whole group went to ensure it was a smooth operation." Carma sits up on the edge of the couch. "I found paperwork that detailed he was the monster who took my sisters. He was known for his perversion. Dwarves and twins and the like. All of my rage and grief was focused on him. Neither of us," pointing to herself and Sabra, "could blame any single person for our losses, until him. This was important."

Carma's demeanor was getting noticeably darker. Ronan knew the end of the story was coming close. He held Taylor's hands tighter, hoping to give him some comfort. "We got to South America safely and found our way to the hidden jungle villa." Sabra says. "As we approached the compound, gunfire could be heard on the horizon. They were fighting amongst themselves. We saw that they were firing between two groups of buildings." He's drawing out the layout with his hands. "We retreated a little way, set up a camp, and waited for the gunfire to cease. Once it quieted down, we waited a few moments to be sure before we sent the first team in. Aleksy was in the forward group as he always was. We were in the rear. They reached one of the houses..." Sabra stopped for a moment. Carma moved closer next to him on the couch. "They went inside the building as we were entering the grounds. I saw his face in the window giving us the thumbs up to come." Carma puts her face into her hands. "The building exploded as we were walking toward it. We were all thrown back off of our feet." The room is completely silent save for Taylor's quiet sobbing. Ronan is stunned by these stories. He'd never heard a story like this and was sad anyone had to actually live it. Sabra finishes the tale "We found no remnants of any one inside the ruins of the building. That day, was the day I renounced any faith I had left. My thoughts of god were reduced to nothing more than a parasite. Sucking the will of people for his own gain, if he exists at all." Ronan was happy to hear him say this, his thoughts were similar. "We traveled back to London to gather our things, chartered a boat to Boston, and have been here ever since trying to survive as normal as possible."

"Wow" Taylor exhales as she rubs Ronan's hand with her thumb. He was so caught up in the story that he didn't realize he was still holding hers. "That is the saddest story I've ever heard. I'm so sorry you two had to live through all of that." Carma replies "We had our good times too and did what we could to reverse some of the damage caused to the world." Sabra chimes in "I'm sorry to bring all of this up but we firmly believe that if more people know what's happened before, we can stop it from happening again. Plus, I wanted you to hear it from us and you should know about our boy. I hope you two can take this story and use it to create a better world. To ensure atrocities like this never happen to anyone else, ever again." The room falls silent in reflection.

Carma breaks the silence "You two best be on home now! It's getting late." She stands and the kids follow suit. "In the name of doing the right thing" She says looking at them "Kiss her already" She smirks. Sabra laughs out loud "Excuse my wife, kids, but she's right. It's pretty obvious." Taylor is blushing for the tenth time this afternoon. "Oh we already got that out of the way" Ronan giggles. Taylor punches him in the arm. "Good! Now get going. We'll see you later." Sabra tells them. They exchange handshakes and hugs as they head out the door.

Once the kids had left, Carma closed the door and looks at her husband. "That story is hard to tell when you're keeping the Angeli parts out." He nods in agreement. "Emma and Henrik haven't told him anything yet. Let's hope he has time to learn of it the right way and isn't thrown in like we were."

"My mind is blown" Ronan tells Taylor as they walk back toward the T station. "That was one of the craziest stories I've ever heard. Can you imagine?" Taylor looks at him. "I can't. I'm so sad for them." He puts his arm around her. "So you know that we're gonna talk tonight. About us." He hesitates towards the end. "I think it's time we do too" She's smiles. "Ok good! I'm starving. Let's get home and see what mom's cooking."

3: EARTH SHATTERING REFLECTION ARISING OUT OF THE BASEMENT

The bell rang like it did every day at 2:37 pm. Ronan's bag was already packed and ready to go. The school days were beginning to kill him as of late. His life had become so much more exciting outside of class that his struggle to care was at an all-time high. He was going to visit the Reis' after school as he did on most days. They had continued to get closer as time went on and they were starting to feel more like family than acquaintances. Taylor was meeting him at their place a little later. She had told him she felt the same way about them. Taylor was meeting with a city social worker after school today for a routine welfare check up. "Unnecessary" he thought but he knew how important paperwork was to the government. Dad's office was covered in it. Everyone could tell she was in such a better place since moving into the Corver's. Her headaches had gone, she was getting better sleep, and she was just all around a happier person. He smiled to himself as he remembered her late night visits to his room. "Those weren't hurting her path to happiness either" he thought.

Ronan navigated through the crowded hallway to their meeting spot near the library and was confused for a moment as he approached. Taylor wasn't there. "She already left for her appointment, ya idiot" he laughs to himself. He couldn't remember the last time she hadn't been standing there waiting with a smile. They met every day and went everywhere together. The plan then came back to him. She was coming to see him at the Reis' after her meeting. He took one last look before making his way outside.

Walking to the Reis' house alone was odd. Today was the first time he'd ever done it by himself. The route to their house hadn't changed though so it was muscle memory and it didn't take very long. He left through the door near the library, he walked down a couple blocks, hit the T station, rode up a few stops, found his way back to the street, and walked down and around the corner to 333. The journey today though, unlike ever before, felt strange. Eerie. He didn't mind traveling alone, so that wasn't it. The street was filled with other people which was normal for the city at this hour, so that wasn't it either. He couldn't place the feeling but he was almost at the Reis' house anyway, so he shook it off.

He approached the steps leading up to the brownstone as he often did. Today though, as If the rest of this walk hadn't been strange enough, he started climbing the steps and noticed the door was open. Even when Carma was outside doing something, the door had always been shut. Panic gripped him and he slowly ascended the stairs and quietly squeezed his head inside. He called out then listened. "Where the hell are they?" He asked himself, worried. There was nothing but silence in the moment after. No one responded but the house was also a literal vacuum. It was completely devoid of sound. He stepped inside, keeping quiet, checking his corners like dad taught him. He reached for the baseball bat they kept near the door and tiptoed in toward the dining room. He immediately noticed the mess. The kids had been helping keep the place clutter free so it was very out of place. As he looked into the living room, it was pretty obvious that someone had turned the place over. The magazines he'd seen Taylor helping Carma organize were scattered and torn in different corners of the room. Other random papers were strewn all over. Even all of Carma's potted plants had been dumped out and thrown around. Someone was looking for something.

His stomach dropped again and he began to frantically search around the main level. He was worried Sabra or Carma might be hurt. When he didn't find anyone, he brought his search upstairs. The upstairs was the same scene of mayhem. Pillows were cut, dressers knocked over. He was having a hard time controlling his worry. His last ditch effort before calling the police, which he planned on doing anyway, was to run downstairs to see what the basement looked like. He was half hoping he'd find them in the house so he knew they were ok but he was also hoping he didn't because he'd be heartbroken if anything had happened to them.

As he opened the basement door, the vacuum feeling hit him at an all-time high. He could feel the silence in the air all over his body. The feeling was nearly indescribable, even though he was experiencing it. Ronan pushed through and made his way down the wooden steps. The further he descended, the worse the feeling was. The air was heavy like water and he noticed he was overcompensating for his steps by not being able to properly feel or hear and that made it difficult to move. Once finally making it to the bottom of the stairs, his despair rose to a dangerous peak. The basement was destroyed. Far worse than the rest of the house. Boxes were crushed with giant slashes through them. Shattered glass and porcelain was scattered all over the floor. He was nervous he'd find them in a horrible way. During his initial assessment of the area, he noticed the metal door cracked open. It looked as if someone had sawed the lock portion right off.

Ronan approached the door very slowly. He was trying to listen for noise inside but still couldn't hear anything but the sound of his own heartbeat. Whatever this feeling was though, he could tell it was emanating from behind the door. He wondered what might be causing it and why it was coming from their son's belongings. He pulled out his phone and kicked the flash light on before sliding the door open just enough for him to squeeze in. He felt like he was walking on sacred ground after the story they had told him about what this place meant to them. Behind the door, a set of stairs brought him lower into the earth. He descended into a room that looked like a spy bunker from the old James Bond movies. The far wall ahead of him was covered with a bunch of paper maps. Strings connected by tacks dotted them. He shuffled further into the room and inspected the radio equipment on a desk in front of the maps. Overhead lights hummed on as he continued forward. "Must be motion detectors." He thought. There was a machine on the table that looked like one of those old phonographs and as he peered at it, he thought that he could see it vibrating. He approached the table and noticed a switch on the side of the device which looked like a power button. He pressed it and all at once, noise came back to him as he dropped to his knees. His instincts had him cover his ears, though he wasn't in pain. The feeling had gone from the air and he could now hear again. After taking a moment to reorient himself, he was able to pick up his phone from the floor and get back on his feet. "This whole thing has gotten very odd." He whispered to himself. The wall to his left was completely covered in weapons. Not guns though. It had swords, spears, pikes, and other weapons of that nature. They were shining and looked like they were in great condition as if they were being taken care of. Taking a closer look, he reached his finger out to touch one of the swords and it cut him. He pulled away quick and stuck his finger in his mouth to catch the blood trickle. Moving away from the weapons so he wouldn't be tempted to do anything else stupid, he spun around to see what else might be in here. Ronan walked around the desk to check out the other wall he'd yet to see. It was very dark in that area so he couldn't tell what was on the wall though he could make out something in the darkness. What he saw when the lights buzzed to life, took the breath from his chest.

As he approached the wall, lights hummed to life revealing a glass case. He wasn't sure exactly what he was looking at but he had a very uneasy feeling about it. Quite simply, he thought they looked like wings. He could tell they were well over seven feet in length based on his own height. He'd never heard of a bird that large though. "What the hell are these things?" He says aloud. As he investigated further he noticed the case had two distinct wings. They were covered in rows of white fluffy feathers like a normal birds only much larger. The top pieces had tendrils protruding from them. "That must be where they connect to whatever they came off of" he whispers, talking to himself. "They're still wet" he added. A loud crash in the basement broke him out of his thoughtful daze. Feeling a little more uneasy about the situation then when he first arrived, he found his way back over to the weapon wall. Quickly perusing the wall, he found a sword he liked the look of. It was a wicked blade. Forged from black steel with a demonic looking cross guard where the grip and blade met. Deep black metal that shined violet in the light curled both over the hilt and the blade. It called to him. After carefully removing the sword from the wall, he held it in his best defensive stance before slowly making his way up the stairs. As soon as he cleared the metal door, it slammed shut behind him. It happened so quickly his heart almost burst out of his chest. He nearly dropped the sword in his surprise. Looking back he thought, "What the hell was that?" A low growl answered his question. Turning back around, warily, his eyes had yet to adjust though he could see something inching out from behind a stack of boxes. Grabbing his phone from his pocket, he shined his light toward the movement and froze in terror. He had never seen something so foul or hideous as this in his life.

This day was turning out to be very indescribable. He could physically see what it was but he having trouble processing why or how it was there. It was semi humanoid in build but had long spiderlike arms protruding from its back. The skin was pale white and gaunt. It appeared that its human arms had been ripped off judging by the bloody bone and sinew left in their place. Its human legs were dead weight dragging behind it as it moved using what looked like spider legs. The fear he felt though, was induced mainly by its face. Its human face was half covered by a black iron mask from the nose up. The mouth had skin stretched between the lips that looked as if they'd been connected but recently ripped apart. At least one row of barbed teeth could be seen through the strings of flesh. The black iron above the mouth had eight orange balls centered in different sizes he assumed these had to be eyes of some sort. It was slowly moving toward him. Finding himself trapped between the door and this thing in front of him, he decided he had no other option but to fight. He wasn't planning on going quietly.

As the creature inched closer, it reared up, showing the full nude body of the human girl. This new standing position shed more light on the creature and Ronan's heart sank into his stomach for at least the fourth time today. The girl had large plump breasts and a tattoo on her left collarbone. It was Lisa's body. Ronan wretched at the thought. "She was annoying as hell but didn't deserve this" he said under his breath. With a heavy heart, Ronan stood defensively, waiting for whatever was going to happen next. He held the sword high to defend himself against the sharp spider legs that were coming toward him. He reached back with his left hand and tried the door to no avail. Ronan would not die a coward so he stood strong, gripping his blade with both hands. He watched the creature inch closer and closer and he readied himself to fight. A sickly sweet smell hit his nostrils and he gagged. He'd never actually smelled it but he read that death smelled similar. The creature spread its top legs out to stop him from getting around it and raised another leg to strike him. As it completed its arc backward and was ready to deliver the killing blow, Ronan swept his sword horizontally, severing the arm. It dropped, sizzling as it hit the ground. A noise like 1,000 maggots being squished filled Ronan's ears and he wretched. Disoriented by the noise, Ronan didn't see the other leg headed his way and was knocked onto the floor. The sword fell out of his reach as he fell. He could now see the noise was the creature screaming and it got louder when another two of its legs were severed. The creature fell to the floor and began writhing. Ronan got up on his feet, grabbing the blade on his way up. He spun around to face the creature, dropping his guard once he saw the man standing on its back, holding a spear that was penetrating the creature's torso.

"Open that door behind you" the man said, pointing to the bunker door. "Quickly." Ronan tried the door again and it gave. He turned to tell the man but fell silent when he noticed the creature starting to glow from the inside. It reminded him of what your hand looked like when you held it in front of a flashlight. The man ripped the spear out of the beast and jumped off its back. Before he could open his mouth to ask him what was happening, the man had him by the arm and they were moving into the bunker. Before he could even blink, he was standing inside the door as it slammed shut in front of him. The man was standing next to Ronan behind the door and crouched down on the stairs, bracing himself. "You may want to get down" He said to Ronan. As he crouched, trying to get his balance, an explosion rocked the house causing him to fall down a step landing on his back. He felt around and sighed with relief as he felt the blade. Propping himself back up, Ronan couldn't help but say "Well shit. I'm pretty confused." "Language." The man said with a stern face. Ronan wasn't sure what to make of him yet. The man was stone faced for another moment but his lips slowly curled into a smile before he let out a loud belly laugh. "I'm kidding. Fuck" He said, smiling. "They call me Shakir. I'm here to keep you safe and bring you to someone with answers, so don't ask me anything." He laughed again. "My girlfriend is on her way here. We need to get her." Ronan told him, worried. "She's already safe where we're going. No worries man. She is actually safer than we are right now so let's get moving." Shakir reached for the iron door but instead of being able to open it, the heavy iron fell outward into the basement. "Well that works too" He said with a smirk. "Oh great." Ronan said to himself with a smile. "Another smartass. I'm used to being the only smartass in the room." Ronan laughed. He followed Shakir out into the basement and was shocked by the warzone. Anything left from the pawn shop was totally destroyed at this point. The explosion had done some damage to be sure but none of the foundation looked damaged so he didn't think they were in any danger of a collapse. "That demon blew up when we killed it?" Ronan asked, inquisitively. "Yeaaaaaaaa" Shakir dragged out. "They all do that. We were lucky this one was small." Thinking about Shakir's words for a moment, Ronan asked "They get bigger than that?" The smirk returned to Shakir's face. "You've seen nothing yet. Sabra's thick iron door saved us. We were lucky this was a fresh one. Had it been older, we might not have made it out alive." Shakir began to survey the basement, leaving Ronan alone to think. "Lisa." He thought. "She must have been following me today." Trying to get this mind off it, he began to play with some sword maneuvers. He got into the zone and felt like he had some semi natural talent at hand to hand combat. Shakir's outburst of laughter brought him back to reality. "Don't hurt yourself Spartacus." He laughed. "You know how to use that thing?" He asked. Ronan chuckled back. "Not really, no, but I won't be caught without a weapon." Shakir nods in agreement before pointing to the exit with his head "Well let's get going before any more demons show up." "That thing was a demon?" Ronan asked, shocked. "Yes, sir." Shakir replied. "No more dallying. Let's get a move on."

The damage from the explosion became more apparent as they progressed toward the staircase. Above them, there was a giant gash in the ceiling that Ronan hadn't noticed before. The house was destroyed. He doubted the Reis' would be back here again anyway. Not being able to wait or wonder any longer, Ronan asked "Do you know what happened to the people who live here?" Shakir stopped and turned to look at him. "They're at command too. Safe, just like your girl. Sorry, I forgot to mention that. Was a little…" He smirked "…Preoccupied. You'll learn everything soon enough." Shakir turned back around and continued the trek forward. "Man, this day has been pretty weird." Ronan said. "You don't know the half of it." Shakir replied. "It's only bound to get weirder for you too so prepare for it."

He collected his thoughts and then warily began following Shakir up the basement stairs. The staircase had clearly suffered damage from the blast but wasn't falling apart yet so he made quick work to climb it, not wanting to be standing on them when they decided to crumble. Once he had reached the main floor, he exhaled a sigh of relief. His relief was short lived though as he took another look around the house. The chaos of the scene had tripled since he first saw it. His heart was so heavy for the Reis', especially after all the work they did together. "At least Taylor and the Reis' are safe" he thought to himself. Shakir was standing near the front door of the house waiting for Ronan. His back was against the wall and his arms were crossed. Donning his perpetual smirk, he said "Look at the door. This is why we can't have nice things." Ronan hadn't noticed until now but the front door was nearly splintered in two up the middle and the bottom of it was blown open. "Where the demon came in?" Ronan asked as he walked over the splintered wood chunks toward Shakir. "Oh I figured it's where you came in!" He replied, laughing. Ronan joined him laughing. "We're going to get along ok." Ronan told him. Shakir came off the wall and dusted himself off. "I was told you were also a smartass." He said. "This could be dangerous, but I'm game." Ronan stepped forward and turned the knob on the front door. The fracture in the wood gave way and the door fell apart, leaving a small section in Ronan's hand. Shakir giggled quietly, but Ronan heard him. As if it had been scripted, the basement stairs finally gave as well and loudly crumbled to the ground. Shakir's giggling turned raucous and Ronan couldn't help but join him. "Are you ready to go see everyone or do you want to break something else before we leave?" Shakir asked through the laughter.

The street was unnaturally clear for this time of day. Sirens in the distance became apparent, getting louder as they reached the curb. "Not looking to have to explain this situation to human cops. Follow me." Shakir told Ronan. They rapidly moved down the empty sidewalk toward the T station Ronan and Taylor used to get here. They round the corner as revved engines and screeching tires turned onto the street. Shakir slowed his pace which made Ronan happy. "I need to get back to the gym" he thought as they walked in silence. They entered the T station and he immediately noticed something different about the inside of the station. It took him a moment to figure out what it was but he realized there were no other people in the station. This station was always packed. "Where is everyone?" He asked Shakir. "They are gone because of us but you're not ready to hear how. Yet" Ronan did not reply. His brain hurt trying to figure out all of Shakir's ambiguous wording. Before he knew it, they had arrived on the platform. They waited by the tracks for only a minute or so before a jet black train car pulled up; completely silent. The doors opened and he followed Shakir into the car. He wasn't shocked to find the train devoid of other people after their last interaction. Shakir sat and relaxed like everything was normal so Ronan tried to do the same. He had no choice but to trust him at this point. The train started to move and Ronan found he was actually able to relax for the first time in a long time. He closed his eyes but couldn't keep the basement scene from haunting him. Something he didn't remember until now was how fast Shakir moved. He'd never seen something move that fast in his life. He opened his eyes once the vision of Lisa played in his mind. Trying to get his mind off of her, He looked over at Shakir wondering if he'd notice anything odd about him. He looked normal by all accounts. Two days' worth of stubble covered his face and his brown hair hung down a little past his eyebrows. His clothes reminded Ronan of Dad's when he was doing training drills for work. Black cargos, combat boots. He had been wearing cut off gloves but had taken them off when he sat down. The hand Ronan could see had a giant circular scar in the middle of it. After the painful story Sabra told him after asking a harmless question, he didn't feel the need to ask Shakir what happened, not yet. He wasn't sure he had the mental capacity to hear that story today.

The ride only seemed to last a few minutes. The windows were blacked out so he had no real sense of where they were or how fast they were actually going but he felt the car starting to slow down now. Shakir stood as it came to a full stop. Ronan stood as well and followed Shakir out of the train. The scene he walked into was not at all what he was expecting and he wasn't sure what to think about it. They were standing on a high platform overlooking a massive metropolis. His first glimpse of the skyline reminded Ronan of the city planet Coruscant. The buildings were lit as if it were the middle of the day but something didn't look quite right as he scanned the horizon. Shielding his eyes with his hand, he looked toward the sun. They were clearly underground which became obvious once he looked closer. The bright ball he had thought was the sun was attached to a giant rotating machine and they were inside of a very large cave. No actual sky was above them. "Where the hell are we?" He asked. "Welcome to Hyperborea!" Shakir answered. "Hyper what?" He asked. Shakir smiled and put a hand on Ronan's shoulder. "I'm the smart ass around here

and I'm feeling a bit challenged but keep it up. It's refreshing."
Ronan smiled back. "This is Hyperborea." Shakir explained. "The
capital city of Thule." "Thule? Like the Thule society? Like the
Nazis?" Ronan asked. "Yesssssssssss and no." Shakir dragged
out. "Follow me this way to your people. I'll let Charles explain
in more detail." "Charles? Who's Charles?" Ronan wondered
out loud. "He basically runs this place." Shakir answered. Just
going with the flow at this point, Ronan followed Shakir down
the steps and onto a skyline walkway. Having asked enough
questions for the day, he followed in silence and made mental
notes of the things he'd want to know about later. They came
upon a house and Shakir stopped in front of the door. "We're
here!" He said. Shakir opened the door and entered. Once
Ronan followed him inside, He saw his parents, the Reis', and
Taylor. He instantly felt a warm relief cover him. This was the
first normal thing to happen to him on this odd day. Another
man was sitting among them. Someone he did not recognize.
Charles he assumed. The man stood and approached them.
With an outstretched hand he said "Good afternoon Ronan. My
name is Charles. I'm very happy you've arrived here safely.
Welcome to Hyperborea." Ronan extended his arm to shake the
man's hand. He looked around to everyone. "What's the
meaning of all this?" He asked. Charles replied "Why don't you
have a seat with your family and I'll try to explain."

4: HYPERBOREA

Ronan's mind was blown. His current physical and emotional state was somewhere between excited and ready to vomit. Was he feeling the need to vomit because he was so excited? He was too busy to worry about the reason. "So let me get this straight" Ronan started with a smirk. "You're all part of some secret multinational society that fights monsters to protect the people of earth?" Charles gave him a smirk back and answered "Well when you put it that way, yes. That's not a false account though it's much more than that." Ronan was having a hard time hiding his excitement. A normal person might be upset, confused, or even scared but this is what Ronan had dreamed of since he was a child. He'd decided the nausea was from the excitement. "So, what does this all mean? Now that we know. Now that we're here." He says pointing to Taylor. Charles looked thoughtful for a moment. "Well your adoptive parents have attempted to keep you safe from this war. They've done a hell of a job until now but since the enemy has discovered you, you're not safe to live your life the way you're used to. The only real option is to bring you in and get you trained as quickly as possible. We can't save you from the war anymore. Your family has an amazing history in this war so we'd love to have you." Ronan's face was full of joy. Charles noticed, smiling as he finished. "We've got some amazing people here to help you two, not to mention the Reis' and your parents." Charles stood and waved Shakir toward the door. "We'll leave you guys to talk and get everything figured out. Henrik, you know where to find me?" Henrik nodded. "Thank you" he said.

"Guys!" Ronan said aloud, directed at everyone. "This is nuts. Like were you ever going to tell me or would you have let my life become something normal and boring?" He sat down with them on the sofa. "Better question, why am I important? What do they want with me?" Henrik stood from the seat and looked to Ronan. "Your parents" He began. Ronan perked up. "They really knew how to throw a wrench into things." Henrik was stone faced as ever. "What he means" Emma also stood "Is that they were also part of our circle here and they fought hard against the enemy. Some resentment still exists I'm sure." Taylor rubbed her hand over the back of his. "So you all knew each other?" Ronan asked. "We did." Emma answered. "Your father and I have been with the Thule since we were born. The Nokmim were recruited long before that. We grew up with the Reis'." Ronan exhaled. "Man, this is just like my craziest dreams come true. I didn't know how I was going to live a normal life. I was dreading it." Ronan told them. Henrik piped up "Don't get too excited until you know what the stakes are. This is a very dangerous time." Emma interjected "Don't stomp on his excitement. I'm glad we can finally bring him into the fold. He may be able to help us end this war for good. It's been hard keeping this all secret too." Ronan stood up and started to pace. The excitement was written on his face. Taylor got up and strolled over to him. "What's going through your head?" She asked. "I'm just thrilled about this. Everything I hoped was real is and we're right in the middle of it!" he told her. "What do you think about it babe?" he asked lovingly, trying to keep her feelings in mind. "Well you guys are my family. I have nowhere else to be and there's nowhere else I'd want to be. This is a little exciting." She smiled.

Ronan stopped pacing and looked toward his family. "I'll let Taylor speak for herself, but I'm in. Not much choice otherwise. Can't go home and I won't sit by and watch." A smirk showed on his face and Emma smiled back as she noticed. "I'm with you guys for the long haul." Taylor said after a brief moment of silence. "We're both pretty athletic. We'll keep each other going." She patted Ronan on the back. Sabra piped in "Aside from the obvious danger of the whole thing, I don't think any of us doubt you two will do great things." They all nod in agreement. "Well, it's decided then. Let's go tell Charles." Ronan directed towards dad. "Ok, let's go get him." Henrik said as he proceeded toward the door. Taylor leaned in to give Ronan a peck on the cheek. "Let's get going." She said to him. "Our new world awaits." Ronan took her hand and they followed Henrik out the door into the bustling underground metropolis. After they had gone and the door had closed, Carma asked Emma "When will they learn the whole truth of this?" "Charles thinks we should fill them in slowly and let *him* tell them himself, when they inevitably meet. Henrik and I agree." Emma responded. "I couldn't imagine trying to process all of this having grown up not knowing." She continued. The room was silent for a moment. Sabra broke the silence. "Max was an amazing contributor to the cause. I see a lot of Max in Ronan. They know he's alive now so we have no choice but to let him prove himself." The women silently nod in agreement. "Plus" He continued "He has someone to help him through. Much like I did." He reached out to touch Carma's hand. "They'll be ok."

The city was an incredible sight to see. They lived in Boston so it wasn't the scale that stood out but you could feel the energy. Nothing like they had ever felt in Boston. The streets and buildings were similar to their city in many ways. Ronan was trying to figure out why it felt different. Dad was explaining the city was very deep underground near the North Pole. If he hadn't seen the giant sun device when he first arrived, Ronan would've thought it was high noon by the seemingly normal summer day that surrounded them. He asked Henrik "Dad, what is that thing? I saw it when I got here but Shakir didn't have time to explain anything." They stopped for a moment and Henrik pointed up to it. "It's not really a sun but you know that. I couldn't tell you the specifics but it's called the Solis. They figured out long ago that it makes it easier for people from the surface to live and work underground if they feel like they aren't. Underground that is." "Interesting" Taylor remarked. "Saying it that way, are there people who live here that you would not call a surface dweller?" She asked. "Oh so you caught that, huh?" Henrik asked. "You'll get all your questions answered soon but to answer that one. Yes. There are multiple species down here." He starting walking again. "Remind me to find out more about the Solis later. I'm interested in the mechanics of it." Ronan said to her. She nodded in agreement and dad laughed. "Just wait kids. I've got a feeling there is much more to come that will make this interesting thing an afterthought."

As they continued their journey through the city, the kids noticed things that seemed out of place. They were small things so neither one mentioned them out loud. People were out living their lives like normal but some of them were different. Ronan was trying to figure out how. A group of young girls sat on a stone fountain they passed by. The girls looked normal by all accounts but a shimmer caught Ronan's eye more than once. He gently nudged Taylor "Does anything about those girls on the fountain seem weird?" She looked hard for a moment and gasped out loud. "What did you see?!" He asked her. "Their skin shines like a rainbow when light reflects off it." "Ok, good" he said, "It's not just me." They exchanged a look and laughed. Henrik overheard and piped in "Atlantians." They answer back in unison with "Huh?" He stopped walking to face them. "Those girls are Atlantians. You know, of Atlantis?" Henrik laughed. Taylor came back with "We heard you" She giggled "but I don't think we were expecting that." Henrik shrugged. "I told you guys you'd see more interesting things." Ronan added "Well you win this round Dad." Henrik smiled. "Like I ever lose. We're almost there." Henrik pointed out "They're expecting us. Let's get over there."

The road they traveled on opened into a bright common area. Groups of people were lounging and chatting which reminded Ronan of Faneuil Hall back home. The landscaping was calling to him. He wasn't a landscaping guy by any means but he couldn't get over how exceptional it looked. Beautiful stone patterns covered the ground and the shrubbery was a vibrant green. As he was looking around admiring the stone work, he saw Taylor's face. She was in awe looking at something too. Ronan followed her gaze to find a full-sized pyramid in the center of the city. His jaw dropped, and he wondered how he missed that. His childhood wonder filled his thoughts and he found himself awestruck for at least the fifth time today. "That's the capital building." Henrik told them, sensing their questions before they asked them. "A fucking pyramid?" Ronan asked, excitedly. "This society is a very old one, son. You've a lot to learn about it yet." Henrik answered. Ronan started jogging toward the pyramid and yelled back "If the reveals keep up in this fashion, I'll never be bored another day in my life." Henrik and Taylor followed him deeper into the square. Taylor's energy matched Ronan's and she ran to catch up. Henrik followed in his usual somber temperament.

Ronan wasn't sure what to expect walking into a pyramid located in a secret underground city. He laughed to himself thinking how he never imagined his inner monologue would be about something like this. Holding Taylor's hand as they walked in, he looked at her and thought how lucky he was she was here to enjoy this with him. Dad was lagging behind the group being the party pooper he normally was. The vibe inside the pyramid was an odd mix of decrepit and high tech. The walls were stone as was the floor but all the fixtures were shiny and black. Ronan felt like he was in the Rebel's base on Yavin 4. It almost perfectly described what he was looking at. They ventured through a set of doors which led them into the command center. Charles was standing with Shakir in a group and waved at them when he noticed they had arrived. People were working behind monitors and running busily around. "They've got a big operation going on down here" Ronan whispered to Taylor as they walked through the room. "So what's the verdict?" Charles directed at the kids as they approached the group. "Everyone is in agreement that joining up is the best option" Ronan replied. "That's wonderful news!" Charles proclaimed. Shakir threw Ronan a look of disgust. "So I guess I'm stuck with you?" He asked. Ronan, full well knowing Shakir was being a smartass, hopped into a fighting stance and punched him on the arm. "And you better get used to it. Quick" Ronan told him. Shakir and the rest of the group laughed.

"What did I miss over here?" A man's voice called out loud enough for Ronan to hear. A few heads turned to see who had joined the group. "Uncle Mason!" Ronan called out, excitedly. Mason approached the group with another young boy. "Hey kid. Glad to see you're finally here." Mason said. Ronan ran up to give him a hug. Once they separated, Mason introduced the boy to Ronan. "This is my protégé Dean. You guys will be training together." Dean reached out a hand to shake Ronan's. "Pleased to meet you. Mason has told me all about you but we haven't been able to meet for…obvious reasons." Dean told him. "I'm glad we're finally able." Ronan waved over to Taylor. He introduced her to Dean as she approached "This is my girlfriend Taylor." He shook her hand as well. "Happy to have some people my age to train with. I'm sick of whooping these old people." The three of them laughed. Mason opened his mouth to say something, but Dean cut him off "I'm kidddddddding, obviously." Mason directed his focus to Taylor for a moment. "Oh Taylor! Wow. I almost didn't recognize you." She giggled. "It has been a while Mason. Nice to see you." She replied. Charles directs toward the kids" Why don't you have Shakir and Dean show you around the city? I'm sure you've noticed a lot of things you'd like a better look at?" Shakir nodded in agreement. Dean verbally agreed. "Sounds good!" He said. "Come on tikes. Let's get it" Shakir said as he started for the door. "Tell mom we'll be home for dinner." Ronan told Henrik. "Be safe guys" Henrik said back.

The group of four reached the exit to the command center and walked out into the warm light of the Solis. "So let me tell you a story" Shakir said to the kids while rubbing his hands together.

5: THE ORIGINAL WORLD WAR

Shakir and the kids departed the capital building and walked back through the beautiful common area. "This is an ancient city and its people are ancient too" Shakir began. Dean added "Like old old." The kids laughed. "We saw some people on our way over that seemed a little off. Nothing bad I mean, but I swear I saw someone blink sideways and another person's skin was shining like a rainbow." Ronan told the group. Shakir laughed. "I'm bringing you guys to the fountain in Sector 2. It's where the locals relax. You'll get some good questions answered today." He told them. Dean spoke up. "The rainbow shine is a trait of an Atlantian." Taylor squeaked out a loud "OH" drawing everyone's attention to her. "So the girls we saw by the fountain were Atlantians?" She asked, embarrassed. Shakir nodded with a smile. "The rainbow shine, as you guys call it, is actually the light reflecting off their scales. Their skin looks like ours though they've got a layer of scales which protects them like armor and makes them fast swimmers." Shakir told them.

The group passed over the bridge which connected the common to the city. This section of the city was called Sector 2, as they had just learned. "How many Sectors are there in the city?" Ronan asked. "Four. Plus the center which is just referred to as the command center." Dean answered. Anticipating a need for more details, he continued. "The Sectors are separated mainly for industry. We don't have problems like segregation down here. We all respect each other for our differences and the strengths we have." Ronan's face lit up. "The more I learn about this place, the more I feel like we belong." Ronan kissed Taylor on the cheek. "So let me try and explain the history of this world. The real history you don't know" Shakir directed to the kids. "With added notes by our other esteemed guest speaker, Dean." Shakir smiled per usual at his own smartass remark. "Hundreds of thousands of years ago, before human existed here, there were other types of people inhabiting this planet. Three specific ones to be exact; The Mu, The Lemurians, and the Atlantians." Ronan and Taylor listened intently. "The Mu lived on a great island in the north Atlantic. They had developed organic flying machines and did most of their hunting and gathering with these devices." Dean interjected "They lived safely in trees that could not be reached without their machines." "I remember reading something about the Mu online but nothing in detail like that." Ronan said. "Well the true history of the world is something of a mystery; half by design, half because time washes away details." Shakir said, thoughtful. He was silent for a moment. Taylor broke the silence "Well that's one of them. Tell us more about the others." "Ooooh right." Dean replied. "Well the Lemurians lived where the Middle East is today. They enjoy being underground. We have them to thank for all of this." He raised his arms up and pointed to everything around them. "They look human as well but their skin is as hard as rocks and they share some traits with reptilians. One such trait being that their eyes blink sideways." Shakir put his hand on Ronan's shoulder. "Any questions so far?" He asked. Ronan and Taylor both shook their head. "No questions" Ronan said "But we haven't heard about the Atlantians history yet. Tell us about where they came from."

"Well they came from Atlantis" Shakir said while turning to watch their reactions, smirking. The kids giggled and he picked back up without their prodding. "Well Atlantis was the grandest city state in this galaxy at the time. It was situated off the coast of Bermuda." Ronan's eyes lit up. "Please tell me it has something to do with the triangle." He said aloud. "The Atlantians think their lost tech is causing the disturbances that make it a dead zone. Yes." Shakir replied. "They haven't gone to find out?" Ronan asked? "That area reminds them of their biggest catastrophe and failure. They steer clear and we don't pressure them otherwise. They've been great allies." Shakir filled them in. "We've had scouts in that area go missing in the past so we all just avoid it. Very powerful tech down there." Dean added.

The group continued small talk while walking until they arrived at the fountain. Shakir directed the kids to take a seat while he and Dean walked toward a small group of people near the water. Taylor gave Ronan a peck on the cheek. "To learn that there is an entirely different history is so hard to wrap my brain around" She said to him. "I'm not having too hard a time. I'm more excited than anything." He said back. "This, I know and could have predicted" She replied with a giggle. "You've always had a different view of how things worked. You were born for this." The guys came back to the bench with another man. "This is Talin." Shakir introduced. "He runs some of our security forces and is an Atlantian. He was there that day and I figured it'd be good to get his take on it." Shakir leaned on the tree next to the bench while Dean and Talin sat on a bench opposite them. "Glad to make your acquaintances." Talin said. "The same to you" Taylor said back. "So where did they leave off?" Talin asked? Ronan replied "They only just explained about the different races. A little about the Mu and the Lemurians. Nothing about your history."

"Well", he started. "It was a couple hundred thousand years ago." The kids looked to each in disbelief. "We were all self-sufficient settlements, but we did trade goods and were very friendly with each other. We mostly kept to ourselves and no one caused any problems. It was as easy a life as I've ever known. One day, seemingly out of nowhere, we couldn't reach the Lemurians while trying to set up a trade deal. We sent a party over to investigate. The scene was chaotic when they arrived. We were under attack from an enemy we'd never seen before. We found out later this enemy was not of this world. The scouts were able to send us a fragmented message as they were being destroyed. We called for the Mu right away to warn them. I personally made that call. The leaders over there had been watching from afar and saw the threat coming so they were already preparing. The Lemurians who were able to escape from their land were on their way to Mu and an offensive was being planned."

"We sent several groups of soldiers to fight though we kept the bulk to protect our own land. I hadn't heard anything directly about what this enemy was but they had wiped out an entire nation of people in what seemed like only a moment. They were monsters, we needed no other details." He paused for a moment. The anger on his face was obvious but his voice didn't show it. "As the enemy closed in on the Mu, they preemptively sprung the attack. It was a useless attempt though. The Mu were also felled. The remaining members of Lemuria and Mu who could escape, did so and came to our land of Atlantis in the south. We had no time to mount any sort of battle plan as the enemy was already on its way to us. We'd been developing a new power source that we determined we could quickly rig into a controlled blast that may stop their battle vehicle. We had the scientists working on that when the others arrived. We explained to our neighbors what our plan was though after seeing the sheer power of our enemy first hand, they saw it as nothing more than an attempted diversion while we escaped. We briefly disagreed until we saw the vehicle of our destruction on the horizon. It was the biggest machine I'd ever seen. The bottom skimmed on the water like a sword tip and it was so tall the top pierced the clouds. We sounded the alarm to evacuate. The Lemurians quickly opened up a tunnel and everyone in the city loaded in. We set the machine to discharge in the direction of the enemy and closed the hole up hoping for the best."

"The group of survivors traveled underground for days. The Lemurians were masters of the ground so the travel was easy. The regret and failure we carried, however, was not. We were heading north trying to get as far away from this enemy as we could. One morning, we eventually arrived inside of a giant cavernous opening." He gestured toward the opening they currently reside in. "The Lemurians had been prepping this area for years and saw fit to share with us. There was running water, being hidden and underground meant we'd be safe from the enemy, and the Lemurians had been developing tech to provide sunlight underground so through our desperation and partnership, the Thule was born. It was the best we had at the time and it ended up flourishing into something great."

"Unreal" Taylor said. "I've never heard of any of this. I can't believe anything like this has actually happened on Earth and no one knows about it." Shakir piped in. "Like I said before, it was a very long time ago. Humans weren't even on earth yet. The bulk of people today have no inkling of what the real world is." Ronan, thoughtful, asked "You say the bulk of people don't know. Who does?" Talin laughed out loud. "Your father was Max right?" He asked. Ronan nodded in agreement. "So I'm told." He said. "I can see the resemblance. Also, nothing gets past you. Max was sharp like that." Talin reminisced. Ronan simply shrugged before Shakir answered him. "High level politicians and religious figures are in on it. Human slaves of the enemy." Both kids had questions but silently contemplated them while Talin continued the tale.

"A few years later, we'd built a great little city. We had no plans to fight, only to survive in peace as we once did. We lived that way until a group of people showed up. They were looking for a safe place to stay. Through discussion, we found out they were part of the enemy species but had been banished for trying to help us. They had also sabotaged the enemy machinery needed to finish their plan for a new race of beings. The beings they spoke of were humans." Ronan was taking everything in the best he knew how and it was a surprisingly easy task. He wasn't shocked about anything anymore; only excited. He did ask questions to make sure he fully understood though.

"So humans were created by these aliens who destroyed your cities?" Shakir nodded his head and replied "Yes. We were created by them. The earth became a farm. Not cattle though, human." "Oh my god" Taylor gasped. "They eat us?" She asked. "Not exactly" Shakir answered while smiling, "but we are grown to nourish them." "But how does that...what?" Ronan asked. Shakir pushed off from the tree and shook hands with Talin. "Thank you old friend." He told him. "Always a pleasure." Talin replied. "Was good to meet you kids. Nice to see you too Dean." Talin continued before taking his leave and rejoining the Atlantians near the fountain. "Let's get headed back" Shakir said to the three. "You'll find out about that later. An Angeli will explain that. One step at a time. It's a lot to digest." Ronan noticed the word he used but left it be for now and the group began their hike back to the Corver's house. "This gets crazier with every second that passes" Taylor whispered into Ronan's ear. "What do you think they mean by we're grown to feed them?" She asked Ronan. "I hope we find out soon." He said. "I'm curious about it too and who these Angeli are."

6: CATHOLIC PROPAGANDA

Rome was beautiful this time of year. Vatican City especially. The air was warm though it was not humid. The breeze brought cool comfort to those caught in its path. The windows could be left open at night and the air for sleeping was beyond pleasant. The smell of the fig trees outside the window wafted inside on the light breeze and helped to mask the sweat and despair that lingered in this particular chamber. Nicola Giordano was lying in his oversized bed, completely naked. He was drenched in sweat and smelled of filth. His nether region especially rank. He had a myriad of slaves at his disposal and had just spent the night raping his two favorite. His slaves were children who were no older than twelve, which was the sweet spot for Nicola. He had worked them long and hard before he had fallen asleep and just finished with one a moment ago. He had realized what day it was and lay in bed, covered in filth and shame, while his thoughts dwelled on his mission today. It was both his favorite and least favorite day of the month. He was to host an audience with an emissary of heaven. This day made him feel very important in the grand scheme but the emissary was terrifying. He'd never admit it to anyone but he felt small and emasculated during the meetings. Coming back to his perfect little reality, a few moments still existed before he had to get ready so he reached around the sheets for the other young boy, grabbed ahold of his privates, and made the moments before he had to get up count.

Once he had finished with the other boy's backside and was overly satisfied with his performance, he rolled off of the poor child, got out of bed, and waltzed into the bath chamber to cleanse and dress with fresh robes. The steamy shower was refreshing after his long night of endless work. After he had cleansed his body, naked, he reentered the bed chamber. The boys had already laid his robes out for him on the freshly made bed. "Grazie" He directed toward the boys. "As you command your holiness" the boys replied in unison. "You boys are so good. Trained very well. It's why you're my favorites." He walked to the boy closest to him and began to kiss the boy on the mouth while holding a handful of hair on the back of his head. Kissing the boy, his erection began to grow. The other boy, knowing what he must do, came over and knelt before Nicola. He grabbed the other boys head and began to inch it closer to his erection. Peering at the clock as the boy's lips brushed the tip of his penis, he stopped the whole affair. "No, my children, no more. I must be on my way. I have a very important meeting to attend. Help me robe up." The boy on his knees let out a quiet sigh of relief and helped his counterpart get the old man dressed.

Nicola, fully robed, headed for the door of the bedroom. He waved goodbye to the boys and exited the room. The guard at the door took Nicola's hand as he entered the hall and kissed it while kneeling. "Your holiness" he began. "I hope to hear your night was splendid." Nicola nodded in agreement. "It was a wonderful night full of pleasure. The one boy though, the one with brown eyes. He has disrespected me and the life I provide them. Make it so I never see him again." Stone faced, the guard asked "Should anyone else?" Nicola clarified. "No, he is nearly too old anyhow." The guard stood and bowed again. He assured Nicola "Whatever you wish your eminence." "I'll return later." Nicola stated as he began moving down the hall. "Bring me a fresh batch of the young ones tonight." He called from the end of the hall. Before he exited, the guard yelled back

to him "They will be here, willing, and ready when you return."
Nicola smiled to himself and thought "They damn well better
be."

As Nicola made his way out of the residence and into
the square, he was greeted by a young cardinal. "Holy father,
what is on the agenda for today?" He asked politely. "I need the
Santa Martha Chapel cleared out at once" He replied. "It's time
for the monthly prayer of intercession." The cardinal perked up.
"At once your holiness" he said as he hurried off. By the time
Nicola had reached the building, it was completely empty save
for the cardinal greeting him at the door. "As requested Holy
Father, completely empty for your use." "Wonderful" Nicola
said. "Now be gone so I may commence." The cardinal perked
up as the Pope entered the chapel before he closed the doors
behind Nicola and breathed a sigh of relief to be rid of him.

The little man scurried down the aisle of the chapel
looking up at the clock. He'd been late to this meeting before
and it wasn't a mistake he was ever going to make again. A
booming voice sent a chill down his spine as it sounded off.
"Just on time I see" The voice said. Nicola stopped moving. "Yes
sir. You know I'm a very busy man down here. Making sure
everything goes according to your plan" Nicola whined in
response while staring at the floor. "Spare me" the voice
replied, bored. A giant frame moved into the light from the
shadows. "All I have to tell you today is that we have an inside
source talking about a plan to attack the Boston Archdiocese in
the near future. Be sure you double the guard. Lose no one and
no information or else it'll be your head that rolls." Sweating
profusely, Nicola replied "Poyel, your excellence, it will be done.
No need to worry." The voice laughed. "I worry not of your fate.
Do not disappoint my father" and with that, a wind took up

making Nicola turn and cover his face. Once it had subsided, the giant was gone along with any dignity Nicola pretended to possess.

Nicola sat on a nearby pew. His false confidence needed a moment to refill. Once he sufficiently felt himself, he hurried back up the center aisle and burst out into the sunlight. The young cardinal, Frank, he believed his name was, stood about 5'5" and was as round as he was tall. He wanted to bring tonight's guests over early because he had a lot of frustration to work out, but he knew that wasn't possible. The young ones were kept off campus to ensure no scandal involving the church should they be discovered. They could only be moved after dark. This fat little man would have to do for now. He was feeling deranged at the moment and hated to take out these sort of feelings on his children anyway so this was a perfect situation. "Cardinal" He barked. "Yes, your holiness?" The young man politely replied. "Come with me to my chambers. I've need of you." The young man perked up. "As you command!" Nicola waved for the man to follow him. As he scurried along the corridors followed by the young man, his mind was running wild with ways to exact his fury on the fat body behind him. The same man was standing guard outside his chamber. "Your holiness! Back so soon?" The guard asked, surprised. "Is my room clear?" Nicola snapped. "Yes it is your eminence. Your guests from last night have been escorted off campus." The guard stepped aside but the Pope grabbed the man's shirt and pulled him closer. "Do not let anyone into this room. No matter what you hear." He released the guard and entered the chamber followed by the portly man. Frank didn't immediately recognize the look the guard gave him as he passed into the

Pope's chamber but he would soon discover it was a wish of good luck.

The door closed behind Frank and clicked locked. He stopped for a moment, unsure of what was happening. Nicola was not in sight but soon strolled out of the bathroom in a silk robe. Frank could make out the entirety of the pope's cock through the robe. It was growing and throbbed as it grew. Frank was mesmerized. "Come down here my son" he said. Frank inched his way down to the main floor of the chamber. "You've never had the lord's blessing from the pope have you son?" Nicola asked him. Frank's face lit up. "No, I haven't your holiness, but am very interested." Frank felt his erection growing inside his robe too. He was both excited and nervous. He was eager to please the pope and was happy he didn't have to hide his homosexual feelings here. Nearly every man in the church was sharing in the lords blessing. Many of the boys didn't enjoy it but Frank did. No one spoke of these feelings publicly so he had to hide the feelings. In this situation though, he felt it was appropriate to be himself.

Nicola motioned the young man toward the bed. "Come lay with me" He said. His outward appearance was calm, besides his raging erection sensing the friction to come. His internal monologue though, was dark. He hadn't quite decided how to carry out his plan yet but he was planned to psychologically break this man before breaking his body. Frank began to shuffle toward the bed. Nicola hopped onto the bed and held out his leg to stop the young man from getting up on the bed. "You must remove your clothes first. No holy robes allowed on this bed." He lifted the robe over his body and dropped it on the floor. Nicola watched as his body becomes exposed and saw his hard cock. His own cock tingled. "Come

show me what you know about the lord's blessing" Nicola
teased. Frank was thrilled and began to lick the base of the
pope's cock before taking it into his mouth. Nicola relaxed while
the young man performed, all the while imagining the countless
ways he could kill this man. Frank took a handful of the pope's
balls and gently squeezed. Nicola was impressed and for a
moment forgot he planned on killing this man. He felt the
familiar tingle in his belly and he stopped the man. "Get your fat
ass up here and show it to me" Nicola told Frank. He smirked
and hopped up onto the bed. He arched his back and readied
himself to accept the blessing.

The pope looked at the scene that is this fat man bent
over. He quickly remembered once he emptied his balls, he'd be
killing this man. He decided in that moment to play nice until he
fell asleep. He wasn't ready to let in on his plan just yet. Frank
wiggled a little and his short erection swayed with his scrotum.
Nicola wanted to finish this off so he got behind the man and
inserted his rock hard cock. "Frank is a hog" he thought to
himself. "He has a tight asshole but the smell was nearly
unbearable." The young man began to stroke his short cock and
as Nicola felt the tingle begin again, Frank began beating more
frantically. When Nicola emptied the content of his balls into
Frank's ass, the young man emptied his balls onto the bed. The
pope rolled off of Frank and lay still for a moment, enjoying his
after orgasm relaxation. "Lay and relax my son" he told him.
Frank was ecstatic. He'd received the lords blessing from the
pope and was now allowed to lay in the holy bed and relax.
Frank rolled onto his side and dozed off a few moments later.

Nicola carefully scooted off of the bed and made his
way to front door. He opened the door slowly, still naked with
his semi hard dick still covered in sweat and feces. "Get me

some strong men and some chloroform to help me get this fat body into my special room." He slammed the door in the guards face before he could answer. Malcolm, the guard, questioned how he got stuck with this job. He began down the hall to call on another couple of guys to help him with the Pope's request.

Nicola calmly strode back down the steps into his room and found his way into the bathroom to wash off the filth. He usually enjoyed the leftovers the young ones left on him but even he was repulsed by this. The pain he was to exact would be well founded on this man. The warm water spurted out as he turned the knob and he furiously cleaned his privates. Grabbing a robe before returning to the bed chamber, he was greeted by Malcolm and two other muscular men. "We've knocked the man out your holiness, would you open the room so we may move him in?" The men bowed awaiting his response. "Oh yes, let me do that for you!" He perked up at the thought. Nicola walked up to a vase on his fireplace mantle and twisted the base which started a grinding. The fireplace began to open until a dark chamber beyond became visible. "Well bring him in!" The pope screamed.

Frank's body was disgusting and the men were not happy about having to touch him but knew they would be subject to this torture if they not obey the orders that had been given. One grabbed Frank under his right arm and the other followed suit on the left, both trying to avoid any part that would be really foul. After getting the best hold they could, they dragged Frank's lifeless body into the secret room. The Pope followed them into the dungeon and pointed to the rack he wanted them to attach Frank to. The men gladly strapped him and were happy to be free of his disgusting body. "Run along now men." The pope shooed them away. "As before, make sure no one bothers me Malcolm." The two muscular men were already headed for a shower while Malcolm walked back to the entrance of the room, turned toward Nicola, and bowed before exiting.

The inside of the room had been crafted after medieval dungeons that the Pope had researched over the years. The room was just beyond his bed chamber but when the door closed, it was a completely different world. The room was covered in stone from floor to ceiling and only dimly lit by torches. Multiple instruments or terror crafted from wood and metal dotted the cavernous room. The walls were purposely thick and built using the principles of acoustics to muffle the screams of the tortured. Nicola would never admit it but he was mildly afraid of the room himself. He only used the room for the serious torture so he wouldn't soil anything in the bed chamber. Cautiously navigating the room to make sure he didn't fall into a trap door, the Pope made his way to the door control.

With the press of a switch, the fireplace closed and sealed the two men in the dungeon. The room became pitch black until the dancing shadows came into view after his eyes had adjusted. The rack Frank was placed in kept him upright with all of his limbs spread. He was still asleep which gave Nicola some time to get things ready. What he had planned was something beyond imagination for normal people. He rubbed his hands together as he got the dopamine tingle up his spine. His cock tingled too. This was one of his favorite things. He wasn't sure how much time he had and wanted everything in order before Frank woke up so he wasted no time.

An altar was set up in the far end of the room. Nicola needed to begin with a part of Frank so he took a small blade and nicked his leg. He collected the blood that flowed out in a ceremonial bowl he was holding. Once he had collected a few drops, he hobbled over to the altar and placed the bowl in the center of the design on the floor. Nicola dropped to his knees and began to speak the Latin verse he had memorized over the years. As he spoke the verse, a light breeze filled the room and the ground began to gently shake. He finished the verse and got back on his feet to move away from the altar as stones began to fall from the ceiling. Slimy tendrils writhed from the newly created hole. A dark blob squeezed out of the opening and landed on the floor with a wet splat. The tentacles of the creature began to spread out and tighten, bringing it to a standing position. A haunting face became present on the front of the beast which shook Nicola to the core. It began to inch its way toward Nicola. He panicked. "Yyyyyoou have the blood of the sacrifice. Gggggggget away from me!" He whimpered. The demon chuckled at the Pope's fright before beginning to move toward Frank's lifeless body. Nicola breathed a sigh of relief as he stepped out of the puddle of piss he had just created. He wanted a better view of what was to come.

As the demon moved toward the unconscious man, it began to take a different form. It became more humanoid while retaining its tentacles. One of these tentacles started moving toward Frank's body and Nicola began to get giddy. He stayed silent to make sure he didn't draw any undue attention to himself. His dick began to get hard as the tentacle took hold of Frank's cock and began to rub back and forth. Frank began to stir. Another of the creature's tentacles came up from behind and slid into Frank's asshole which was met with a groan. Nicola began to touch himself as he watched. Frank started to moan which led the pope to believe Frank was semi awake and

enjoying it. He was growing impatient but knew a demon's goal
was to confuse and terrify a person before killing them so he
continued to stroke though he slowed down. He wanted to
finish at the same time Frank's life was finished.

The demon moved in front of Frank and the noise that
came out of Frank's mouth was one Nicola had never heard
before. A chuckle that sent a shiver down Nicola's spine came
from the demon as its other tentacles began to spread out and
pulsate. The pope began beating faster. The rack Frank was
attached to had him held tightly. He was trying to get free as
the demon continued to stroke his cock and thrust the tentacle
in his ass. Two tentacles wrapped around Frank's arms and
ripped him free from the rack. The demon raised him into the
air and pulled tight to hold him. Frank moaned and shook as if
he was having an amazing orgasm and Nicola stopped stroking
for a moment. He was close to finishing. The rest of the
tentacles began to move and he screams out a singular word,
"DAD", before a tentacle entered every hole on his body and
began to fuck. The pope moved toward the front of the
spectacle to make sure he can see the carnage. He could see
from his new vantage point all the gruesome details. Tentacles
were in his eyes, ears, nose, mouth, cock, and ass. It was a
brutal sight. He knew it was painful and as blood poured from
Frank's body, Nicola emptied his balls onto his hands. Frank was
dying a slow and painful death in front of him and he wished he
could get off again. The body stopped moving momentarily and
with what could be best described as a grunt, the demon
tightened all the tentacles inside of the body and ripped Frank
into pieces. A warm blood mist sprayed across the room
covering Nicola and everything else in it. Nicola's balls tingled
and he came again, standing there naked covered in blood.

After a moment of Euphoria, fear creeped into him. The demon was free of its mission now that Frank was dead. He moved back until he hit the wall. He wanted to ensure the demon didn't need to pass near him on its way back to the portal.

It turned back into its blob shape as it slugged back toward the altar. Before entering the portal, it grabbed a chunk of Frank's body and hurled it toward the pope. The demon chuckled with delight as Nicola screamed like a girl and lost his bowels on the wall. With no further ado, the demon returned to where it came from and the hole closed behind it. Nicola breathed a sigh of relief it was gone. He was covered in blood and shit but he was alive. He started for the dungeon exit but stopped when he saw Frank's head on the ground. Wanting to complete his humiliation, he plucked the head from the ground and wiped it in the fecal matter on his back side. After he determined it was sufficiently covered, he walked it over to his pile of cum on the floor and dropped the head into it. "Fat fuck" he thought to himself as he booted the head against the wall watching it splat when it hit.

The only time Malcom enjoyed his job was at times like these. The Pope's chamber was silent and no one had passed in the hallway for clear over an hour. Peace and quiet here meant no dirty deeds for him to carry out. He often thought of his childhood and how happy his family was that he had agreed to go into the service of the church. Little did they know he had willingly agreed to go into service of the church because he had heard whispers of what it meant to be an actual part of the church. His childhood friends included a young boy who had escaped from the Vatican. None of their parents knew about Vasili but he was a good friend growing up. He had a nice little place off the Via Della they would gather to play. The boys brought him food and blankets when they came to visit. He didn't talk much about his time inside the Vatican but the stories he told the group still haunted Malcom to this day. They hurt worse now because he knew they were true. He remembered how afraid Vasili was to be found. He constantly felt like they were looking for him. The boys tried to comfort their friend but one day they came to his spot in the alley and he was gone. They returned for a few days after hoping to see him but they eventually stopped when he wasn't there. Malcom kept coming back for some time. After a couple of months had passed and Vasili was nowhere to be found, he told his mother he wanted to go into church service. He'd worked here since he graduated the academy. "It's me or them" he told himself as some sort of mantra. He was jarred back to reality as the door behind him clicked and opened.

Nicola strode out into the hallway, naked and covered in all sorts of filth. "Have my dungeon cleaned up before I return from evening mass. It is a mess!" He stormed back into his room and slammed the door. Malcom waited a moment to react while he fondly remembered his friend. After another moment or reflection, he reluctantly made his way to the office to enlist some help for the cleanup effort. He followed his orders well. He knew firsthand what happened to people who crossed the church.

7: THE REVELATION

Ronan noticed the Solis machine moving downward as they walked. "Oh wow" He thought to himself. "It sets too." Shakir struck up conversation as they strolled through town. "There's still so much more to learn about your past and the history of the world but how are you guys taking it so far? I know it must be a little unnerving." He smiled. "I remember when I was brought up to speed." Ronan answered him first "I've always felt a little off. Special comes to mind though I don't want to come off cocky. Thinking about working forty hours a week and paying bills until I died scared me more than any of this does. I'm ok with it all so far." Surprised, Dean commented "You guys worry about weird things on the surface." The group laughed. Shakir asked once it had gotten quiet "What about you Taylor?" She took a moment before responding. "These guys are the only real family I've ever known. I'm happy to be with them. Some of this stuff is really stretching my reality but as long as I'm with them, I'll make it through." "Glad to hear." He replied. "I'm sure dinner will hold some new surprises. Be ready." He warned. Ronan grabbed a hold of Taylor's hand "We're ready" he proclaimed. Shakir smiled as they turned a corner onto the side street the Corver's house sat on.

Ronan was the first one through the door and was elated to see that everyone was here for dinner. "Hey everyone" He called out. Mason and Carma greeted them from the dining room. "The rest of the men are playing chess in the other room" Carma told them. Not wanting to disturb the game, he b-lined for the kitchen. "Whatcha making Ma?" He called to Emma as he walked through the dining room, Taylor in hand. "Come in here and find out" She called back with sass. As they entered the kitchen, he couldn't help but smile. "Lobster mac and cheese?" He asked. "Damn right." She replied. "We're right under the arctic ocean here. Some of the best crustaceans around." She licked her lips. The kids laughed. "I'm fine in here" she said with a peck on both kids' cheeks. "Go help Carma set the table" She directed. "It should be ready any minute." They followed her direction and left the kitchen to help get ready for dinner. When they got back into the dining area, the table was already set and Shakir was sitting down, anxiously awaiting the food. "Why don't you two go round everyone up?" Carma suggested with a smile. Taylor answered her "Ok. We'll get them!" Charles and Sabra were still locked in a banging game of chess in the next room when the kids entered. Sabra looked up at them. "Hi kids!" He said, excitedly. "Foods ready!" Ronan directed at the both. Charles replied "It's about time. I'm starving!" He looked to Sabra. "Pick back up after dinner?" He asked. "You know it!" He answered.

Everyone gathered in the dining room, anxiously waiting the feast to come. Taylor was thrilled. She always enjoyed moments of family bonding like this. She didn't have many from her childhood. She reached over and pecked Ronan on the cheek. "I love you" She whispered into his ear. He smiled and whispered back "I love you." Charles, stuffing his face with garlic bread, directed to the kids "So Shakir tells me you guys are taking all this new information well." The kids nod. "This is what I'd always hoped for" Ronan stated. "I'm thrilled it's happening." Taylor spoke up after. "Totally blowing my mind but I'm with my family so it's doable." Charles looked pleased. "Good. Glad to hear. Are you ready for some more?" Ronan looked at Taylor. "I'm ready. What about you?" He asked her. She replied "This is all about you babe. If you're ready, I'm ready." Charles nodded and began. "Have you ever wondered about your family?" He directed at Ronan. "My biological family?" He clarified. "Yes. I know the Corvers have been with you since you were an infant, but your own family history has an unbelievable story." Ronan squirmed in his seat. "Wow." He said aloud. "I never thought I'd be hearing this." "Brace yourself." Charles told him. "It's wild".

"Your grandfather was a Hauptmann in the German Army." Ronan gasped out loud. Sabra added to the tale. "Now you mustn't think poorly of him. It was not something one chose in that time, it was something one must do to survive. He was not involved in any of the genocide projects. He was a brilliant strategist on the battlefield." Taylor rubbed his hand under the table. "We worked with Hans for many years after the war. He was a standup gentleman." Sabra finished. Ronan spoke up. "I'm glad to learn he was a nice person. The stigma overtook me there at the beginning." Charles nodded. "You'll find out many disturbing facts during your time with us. Things are not as you think a majority of the time. Be sure to learn the whole truth before coming to judgements." Ronan acknowledged Charles before he continued. "Hans was among Hitler's party that escaped after the fall of Berlin. They managed to find their way to Argentina, where they began to devise a plan to fight back." Taylor interjected "Didn't Hitler die in Berlin?" "He wanted people to think so." Charles answered. "The Hitler you know, is not the man who arrived in Argentina. The Hitler you know was possessed by the enemy. He, much like your grandfather, is a standup gentleman. A lot of this is thanks to him." Ronan looked to the Reis'. "So the camp you guys found was this one? My grandfather was there?" Carma answered him. "He was in the house with Aleksy." "Oh no"

Taylor gasped. Charles began again. "Do you see how all of our fates are intertwined?" Ronan nodded. "So what of my mother and father?" He asked. "Well Hans made many trips back to Europe as part of their preparation. Apparently, he met a wonderful young Czech girl on one of these trips. Your father, Max, was born in 1965. When he was a young man, he set out to find who he was. He ended up joining the Nokmim with these fine folks here." Taylor asked, "So you guys knew his real father?" Henrik answered her question. "We were the best of friends. We all grew up together." Ronan asked excitedly "Well what happened to them? My parents?" The table went silent.

Charles began after a moment of silence. "We got word of an impending global attack on humanity. Just before the turn of the century." "The attack on America and the war that is still raging?" Taylor asked. Shakir nodded and picked up the story. "Our forces have always been dwarfed by theirs, but we try anyway. Every time we can. As you both very well know, this mission was a failure. Your parents, Ronan, were among the group we took to Afghanistan. You were only an infant." Shakir stopped and Mason started. "The enemy had taken control of a native leader and was rallying a force to do damage and start another world war." Emma picked up the story from here. "We ended up finding the man we were looking for, but he knew we were coming. There was a very large force waiting and traps had been set. We came prepared, but we still lost a few good people." Sabra added "These caves were among some of the first places on this world touched by the enemy. Your parents were hit by a blast, but we never found their bodies. We can only assume they were thrown into some sort of dimensional shift left over from when the enemy had been there in ancient times." Charles finished this part. "We can't confirm they're dead, but we haven't heard from them since that day. No one knows where that portal could have led. Emma and Henrik took you in when we returned." Ronan stood from the table. "So, there's a chance they're alive?" He asked rather loud. Charles answered "Like Sabra said, we never found their bodies, but we fear the worst. That portal could have led anywhere." Ronan nodded in acknowledgment. "Such an odd feeling." Ronan started. "Knowing who they are. Knowing they're not confirmed dead. It's a glimmer of hope. I never knew if they just abandoned me and were out there somewhere or dead. Never really cared. Now, the same facts that damn them might be their saving grace. We don't know where it went. They might be alive somewhere." Taylor rubbed her hand over Ronan's back. "I like the way your brain works" Charles told him. "I'm glad you're here with us. Reminds me of when we had your parents here. It was a simpler time." Charles reflected internally for a moment. "Do you have any other questions about what we've just told you?" Ronan looked around the table "What is my mother's name? And my family name?" Emma stood and answered. "Your parents were Lukas and Asuka Lorenz. They were good people and good friends." The table went silent in reflection once again.

Carma stood and asked for help clearing the table. Shakir, Charles, Mason, and Dean volunteered following her lead. She directed toward Ronan and his family "Why don't you go into the den and talk about this some more?" Taylor stood and grabbed his hand. "Come" She said. He stood and followed her into the other room. The Corvers excused themselves from the table as well. "Charles" Shakir said after the Corvers had left the room, "This seemed to hit him hard. We should give them some time before we go any deeper. Their training should still

start tomorrow though. We have a lot of time to make up for."
Charles patted him on the back. "I agree. Let's get them up to
speed on fighting. There will be more time to discuss the truth
of all of this later."

Entering the room first, Ronan and Taylor sat on the
large fluffy couch near the fire. Emma and Henrik followed
shortly after and took a seat on an adjacent couch. Taylor
snuggled in next to Ronan and he snuggled back. She was
thankful for times like this. Emma asked, "So where's your head
at boy?" He thought for a moment before answering. "I never
really thought about them. I never asked because I was afraid of
what I'd be told. Car accident, drug overdose, or worse, they
just left me." He stopped for a moment. "Now, I find out about
how crazy my family's history is and that there's a chance
they're alive!" He was excited. "I just don't know what to think
but it makes me want to be a part of whatever this thing is. All
of my family has been, and it may lead me to finding them or at
least finding out what happened to them." He relaxed a little.
"So, I'm in a weird spot but I'm with you guys. I'll be fine!"
Taylor spoke up. "I couldn't imagine finding out something so
crazy about my life!" "What do you know about your parents?"
Henrik asked her. "Absolutely nothing" She replied. "My very
first memory was in a group home." "That's very sad to hear"
Emma said to her. "You know you're as much a part of this
family as anyone?" She asked Taylor. "I've never felt more at
home than with you guys" Taylor replied. Ronan piped up "I'm
tired guys. I want to go lay down." Taylor nodded in agreement
and stood with him. "Get some good rest tonight. They plan on
bringing you to class tomorrow." Henrik told the kids. "What
type of class?" Ronan asked. "A crash course into the real world.
Nothing like the history you've been learning. More physical."

Henrik laughed. "Oh boy" Taylor said, "More surprises." They all laugh as Emma stood and gave them both a kiss goodnight. "See you in the morning" She said.

The kids left the den and ran into Dean waiting for them in the hallway. "Hey guys, got a minute?" He asked them. "Sure do!" Ronan answered him. "This whole thing just sounds oddly familiar to me." He started. "My parents were killed on mission when I was an infant. Mason took me in." Taylor gasped. "So, we're all in the same position" She said. Dean nodded. "That's what I was thinking. I know we're from two different worlds but I'm offering myself to you guys. Let me help if I can. Let's teach each other and stick together. Being able to relate to each other on this level is refreshing. I've never really been able to." Ronan put his hand out to shake Dean's. "Sounds good to me man" Ronan said as they lock hands. "I've got a feeling there's a lot coming, and we may need all the help we can get. Not sure how we'll be able to help you though." Dean laughed. "I don't go up very often, so I know very little about life upstairs. I feel out of place because most everyone else is from up there originally. I just want to feel like I fit in." Taylor put her hand on Dean's shoulder. "We will definitely get you up to speed." Dean smiled big. "Great guys! Happy we got to catch up. I'll meet you tomorrow morning for training. Have a good night." Dean took his leave, rejoining Mason in the dining room.

The kids followed him into the dining area to say goodnight to the rest of the group. It seemed that Shakir and Charles had already left. "Good luck tomorrow you two!" Carma tells them. "But we don't think you'll need it" Sabra said with a chuckle. "Thank you" the kids replied in unison and waved as they go back to the hallway and start up the stairs. "Ms. Quinn" Ronan said as he took a handful of butt. "Want to help me get to sleep tonight?" He whispered into her ear. She gently grabbed hold of his privates and whispered back "Lead the way."

8: THE BEGINNING OF HIS THULE ACTIVITIES

Ronan woke that morning feeling well rested. He carefully rolled over to gaze at Taylor. She was still sleeping peacefully, and he couldn't help but think how cute she was. He gently ran the back of his hand over her cheek and she slowly opened her eyes with a smirk. "Good morning beautiful" he told her. "Good morning handsome" she replied. "It's time to get going. We're meeting Shakir over at the training facility in a little while." Ronan reminded her. "We have time for a shower?" She asked. "Yes ma'am, let's get to it though!" He said excitedly as he got out of bed. He made his way into the bathroom and turned to watch her beautiful little body follow him in.

After the shower, the kids walked back into the bedroom. Clothes were laid out waiting for them that weren't there when they had gotten up. "Where'd these come from?" Taylor asked. Ronan noticed a sticky note on them. "You'll be happy to have these. Thank me later. –Dad" Ronan read aloud. "Well that was nice of him!" Taylor said. The spread was black combat pants with built in knee protectors, black combat boots, and tight fitting black shirts that looked rugged with some armor padding built in. Ronan picked the shirt up "They did say we were training in combat." He laughed. "These should help keep our bodies from bruising. I doubt we'd feel a thing wearing these." She walked over to the bed and grabbed her pants. Ronan watched Taylor as she pulled the pants up over her thighs and wiggled her butt into them. "Damn girl" He said, "You're hot." She blushed and giggled. "I'm glad you think so, but you better hurry up and get yours on too, we're gonna be late!" He snapped out of his lust filled haze and raced her to catch up.

Emma had a full breakfast spread on the table waiting for them when they got downstairs. "You're going to need to eat good this morning" She said as they come into the dining area. "Thanks Ma" Ronan said followed by a kiss on the cheek. Taylor came and gave her a hug too. "I'm starving" Taylor admitted. "Today is going to be a weird day for you both. You're going to learn more truths that may make you question everything you know." "Damn" Ronan replied. "Anything like what we found out last night?" Emma smiled and said "It's not anything to do with anyone personally, so no. It's probably more fantastic and extraordinary than what you learned last night so…be prepared." Taylor made a surprised face "Well now I'm pretty interested to know." Ronan looked at her. "Me too. I'm loving this life of secret and intrigue. Better than fifth period math class, for damn sure." They all laughed. Emma looked at the tIme "Ok, sit and eat you two! You're meeting Shakir over at the command building soon." They drop into the chairs and start loading up their plates. Emma asked, "You remember how to get there, right?" Ronan nodded his head while shoveling French toast into his mouth. Once he swallowed he replied "Yea I do. Down past the fountain. It's pretty much a straight shot from here." "Great!" Emma said. "I'll see you at dinner. Now get going" She shooed them out the door, giggling.

The walk this time around was completely different. They had always had a guide focusing their attention before today but now making the journey alone, they were able to fully enjoy the sights and sounds the city had to offer. The commute didn't take very long as they were both eager to see what the day held for them. No one had been very clear about what the training was so the curiosity was a burning a hole in both of them.

Before it felt like the walk even begun, they had arrived in the common area outside the pyramid. Ronan stopped and kissed Taylor on the cheek. "You ready to do this?" He asked her. "Ready as I'll ever be" She said. They entered the massive pyramid together and found Shakir waiting for them just beyond the entrance. "Good morning love birds." He said with a fake smooch. Taylor blushed, and Ronan gave her butt a playful smack. "Jealous?" He asked and laughed. "I'd be if I were you. She's lovely." Ronan said. "She is a fine woman." Shakir told him. "My heart... was... lost long ago... but enough of that nonsense, are you two prepared for this?" Ronan jumped into a play fighting stance "You bet. Bring it on." Taylor promptly nodded. "Great. Follow me to meet your instructors for the day." Shakir waved a hand to follow as he turned and began walking. Beyond the control room they'd visited before, a large set of stairs led to a lower level. They followed Shakir down the steps and through large wooden doors. The room they entered was a massive oval with a section of turf in the middle set lower than the rest of the room. A group of people could be seen sparring on the turf and there were many other people around the room doing various other busy tasks.

"Shakir?" Ronan said to get his attention. "Yes, my sweet" He responded sarcastically. "Where is Dean?" He asked, laughing. "He told us we'd see him here this morning." Shakir stopped and turned to the kids. "Mason and Dean actually left on an emergency mission late last night. They'll be gone for some time." He picked his pace back up and they followed. "Bummer" Ronan said to Taylor. I like him. "I did too" She said. "Hope they'll be ok."

One of these men noticed them arrive and gleefully walked over to greet them. He was average height and build. No features stood out about him except his outdated clothing. He was dressed like an extra from a period film set in the 1800's. Ronan spied a nice velvet jacket and a top hat near the desk the man had come from. "Shakir!" The man called out with distant British flavor. "Victor" He replied with a firm handshake. "These the kids?" Victor asked. "Yes. Ronan and Taylor" Shakir pointed out. "Very good. Follow me to my area over here children. We have much to discuss." Victor directed at the kids as he began to walk. "I'll be around if you guys need anything. Pay attention. This stuff will save your life" Shakir told them as they began to follow Victor.

They arrived at the area Victor mentioned and he pointed out a couple of desks adjacent from an old blackboard. Ronan giggled to himself. They had old wooden desks, he was in a great looking suit, and he used chalk on the blackboard. Taylor took a seat at one of them. "Victor" Ronan called his attention. "Yes?" Victor answered. "Tell us a little about yourself. I'm meeting lots of new people and I'm enjoying finding out about them." Victor nodded. Taylor looked to Ronan and silently mouthed to him "What are you doing?" Ronan smirked at her and gestured toward Victor with his eyes. "Sure thing" Victor answered out loud. "Please have a seat and get comfortable!" Ronan settled in at his desk. "Give me just a moment kids" Victor said before walking over to Shakir. In a whisper, Victor tells Shakir "He's asking about me. I believe he's put it together already. Color me impressed. Are they good for the truth?" Victor asked. "As far as it goes with your story. Yes. They're good." Shakir answered. "Try to leave any of the bigger stuff out if possible. They've only been with us a few days. Took us hundreds of years to get acclimated." Victor nodded in agreement. "Duly noted, sir."

Taylor whispered to Ronan "What'd you think they're talking about?" He shrugged his shoulders and shook his head. He noticed Victor coming back over and focused his attention. "Ok Mr. Corver's, Ms. Quinn, as you're seemingly very intelligent of the situation here, I've been cleared to tell you about myself." Ronan deviously smiled. "I was born in Napoli to a loving mother and a very stern father. I grew up with two brothers among a couple of adopted sisters. Before leaving for university, I lost my mother to scarlet fever. Her death drove me to study science and chemistry and I did just that. I graduated from the University of Ingolstadt and became a registered doctor." Ronan chimed in. "Victor, you say you went to the University of Ingolstadt?" "Yes, that is where I obtained my degrees." He answered, smiling. Ronan continued. "The university closed around, what, the year…eighteen…hundred, if I remember correctly?" Ronan asked. Taylor's face turned white. "I do believe it did. That sounds correct, though I graduated some years before that so I'm not positive."

Ronan looked to Taylor. She looked as if she'd seen a ghost. "What… is… going… on?" She asked. "I've had an odd feeling about this whole thing." Ronan answered. "Looking at him when we got here, added to the things we've been learning about, really got me thinking. My hunch turned out right. Victor," Ronan asked, "How old are you?" Victor thought for a moment. "246 years old if my math is correct and that's not really ever in question." He smirked. Taylor's disbelief was apparent. "How is that even possible? You look like you're barely thirty" She said loudly. "That my dear, is a story for another day! Now are you two ready to begin with the lesson?"

Victor asked. "Yea, I think I'm ready. Very curious to see how this all plays out." Ronan said with a smile. He rubbed Taylor's back and whispered into her ear "You good babe?" She nodded "I'll be good. I should stop being so surprised about everything. Crazy is normal down here." "You can say that again" He agreed.

Victor began his lesson for the day explaining how the Thule ecosystem functioned. He explained how every tree and plant on the earth's surface was a conductor of energy generated by the sun. The Lemurians had crafted a process to harness this power some millennia ago for a multitude of things, the Solis machine being one. It replicated the sun's properties in a much smaller capacity, so life could flourish underground. Plants were large and vibrant, the air warm and habitable, and there was a night cycle so sleep patterns were not affected. "So, that sun outside is a giant machine that's powered by actual solar energy?" Taylor fact checked. "Yes, ma'am. That is precisely what powers it" Victor answered. Ronan asked, "What else is the energy used for?" Victor smiled big. "I was hoping you'd ask." He spun around and pulled a chart down from a rollup above the blackboard. There were a few diagrams scattered about the sheet. One looked like the sun and the ground. The colony was also depicted below that. It showed how the sunlight is transferred from the roots to storage tanks below ground. There was also a diagram of a human body. Before Ronan could ask about it, Victor began explaining. "So, as you know, the solar energy powers the Solis device but it also powers basically everything else. The lights, the water pumps, our vehicles. Even us!" He pointed to the body diagram. "I've synthesized an antidote for... eternal life." He said the last words as if he'd never had to explain it in this way before. "So that's how you're still alive?" Taylor asked, unintentional surprise in her voice. "That it is Taylor. I was brought on board due to certain…scientific studies that I conducted in my youth." Ronan butted in "You created life, right?" Victor looked stunned for a moment before regaining composure. "You, sir, are more perceptive than anyone has let on. I'll be keeping my eye on you. You're going to do great things." Taylor, dumbfounded, asked "What're you guys talking about?" Ronan smiled at Victor and he nodded with approval. "This is Victor Frankenstein." Ronan told her. "He's real?!" She asked, rather loudly. "I thought it was just a story." Victor piped in. "I'm very real, I can assure you. That nasty harlot Shelley stole my journal from me, however, and made my life into that melodramatic romance tale you've read." The kids laughed. "So, you're real, what of your monster?" Ronan asked. Victor perked up and yelled "Alphonse!"

The kids turned in the direction of Victor's gaze. A hulking brute of a man was walking toward them. His footsteps were loud pounds on the floor. Every part of his body was extremely large. He looked like a seven-foot-tall strongman competitor. Taylor grabbed a hold of Ronan's thigh and squeezed. She was nervous. Once he came into view, she released her hold. Despite his size, he was a normal looking person. He was easily the biggest human Ronan had ever seen. His head was bald, and he had some faint scars over his face but couldn't be described as a monster by any meaning of the word. Victor introduced him "This is my lifelong companion, Al. Named after my father. He is the man I created after college." Taylor and Ronan stood up to shake his hand and introduce themselves. "Very nice to meet you both" He said. His voice was very baritone but also normal by all accounts. "I can see you're

a little shocked. Most people who've read that terrible story
are. I can assure you I'm as normal as someone could be,
reaching over 200 years of age and having been brought to life
in a laboratory." He laughed. The kids joined in. "I am at your
service young masters. Please do not be afraid to ask anything
of me." He bowed toward Victor and returned to his previous
task.

Nonchalant as can be, Victor said with a smirk "May we
continue with the lesson now?" The kids agreed and sat back
down to listen. Victor pointed back at the body diagram. "I had
very crude ideas and formulas back when I began. Once I was
approached by the Thule, I had access to more advanced
technology and was able to synthesize my elixir from the Solis
energy. The form of the elixir used for life we call Vitae. It
increases speed, strength, and cognitive ability as well. Ronan
chimed in "It's all coming together now. Is it also the cause of
the glowing eyes?" Victor nodded and smiled. "Very good
Ronan. Indeed, it does." Taylor asked, "Do we get to use this
formula?" "I've got Al preparing yours as we speak" Victor
replied. She wondered "Does it hurt? I'm a little nervous."
Victor assured her "It's quite comfortable. You'll feel no
different once it is administered. You'll then begin to notice
you're very fast and very strong. Your mind will begin to work
more clearly and you'll never age! It's actually quite brilliant."
"Well I'm ready!" Ronan said. "As I knew you would be my boy"
Victor answered.

Shakir entered the classroom area with Al and another
man they'd yet to meet. "Ok kids, Victor's gone over this *magic
elixir* of his right?" He laughed. "Yea he has. Is that it?" Taylor
pointed and got up to see what Al was holding. Ronan followed
her over. "It looks like liquid sunlight" Ronan mentioned to

Taylor. "That's it. That's the magic elixir" Shakir told them. "You ready to get this out of the way? Live forever like us?" Ronan grabbed Taylor's hand. "I mean it's an odd thing to be ready for, but yea I am. Let's do it." Taylor nodded. "Ready as I'll ever be." She said. "Fantastic! Al, bring those here if you please." Victor asked. Al handed the tray holding the syringes to Victor. He placed them on his desk. "Come over here kids. Roll up your sleeves. Victor cleaned a spot of skin with an alcohol pad and administered the Vitae. Once it was released into her veins, she thought she could see her veins glowing. It was as unpleasant as any other shot she'd received but not any worse. "You kids are good to go!" Victor told them, putting down the syringe on the tray held by Al. Shakir came up to them and placed his arms around their shoulders. "Welcome to the team. Officially." He said. "Vitae enhanced humans are amazing in battle. It's time to see what you've got." He walked over to the other man and patted him on the shoulder. "This is Attila. He's going to show you how to use this new-found strength and speed to whoop some tail." Shakir laughed. Attila was a short man. Very stocky but muscular. He had an amazing moustache and thick black hair, braided. Ronan couldn't hold back his laughter. "Knowing what I know, this is Attila? Like the guy who climbed the Great Wall and battled the Chinese?" Attila nodded, never changing his stern expression. "That was a lifetime ago, but I learned many things through the years that make me useful here. You'll find most of us have… interesting… past lives but we come together here to administer change. You will learn to fight with me and you will be the best because of it. Come." He beckoned them to follow him to the turf in the lower section of the room. "Your bodies will hurt but you will be ready to battle." Attila warned them as they followed him to the field. He reached into a weapons rack and threw two wooden poles at them. "Do as I do, and you will survive the war to come."

Ronan's arm moved faster than he realized it could and he expertly caught the weapon as it came into reach. He looked to Taylor and she had done the same. He looked as surprised as he felt. "The serum fast at work." Victor called from the spectator position above the field. A note of excitement in his voice. Ronan caught movement out of the corner of his eye and turned his head to see what it was. Attila was coming at him with his weapon ready to strike but was moving in slow motion. Ronan just stood still, confused, and watched as Attila slowly made his approach. He waved his arm and noticed he was still moving at normal speed, so he turned to see what Taylor was doing. She was also moving in slow motion. He kept his gaze on her for another moment, admiring her. "What're you looking at punk?" She startled him when she spoke, and he jumped. Before he answered, he checked on Attila again who was still moving extremely slowly. "Are you seeing this too?" He finally asked her while pointing at the slow-moving warrior. "Yea I am. Victor said this is the Vitae?" She asked. Thinking the situation through, Ronan responded "We must be moving really fast. That's why everything else seems to be moving slowly." Taylor's face went blank for a second, thinking about it. Ronan looked back to Attila who hadn't moved very far up to this point. "Don't you think Attila also has Vitae? Why isn't he...?" Ronan was cut off mid-sentence as a wooden pole contacted the back of his shins and swept him off of his feet. Taylor saw him go down but before she could react, was knocked sideways by the same pole.

Laying on the ground, in pain, the kids sat up to see what happened. Attila was leaning on the pole in his hands, smirking for the first time since they had met. "Regardless of the situation, never let your guard down. Rule #1." Ronan got to his feet and helped Taylor up. "Interested by your new speed?" Attila asked. "Very." Ronan answered while dusting himself off. "Pick up sticks. Let's continue."

The next few weeks saw Ronan and Taylor continuing to learn theory from Victor and training with Shakir and Attila. Their bodies were bruised but their spirits were renewed and their minds sharp. They fit in perfectly with the group and were anxious to become useful members when the time came. Ronan wondered what the next shocking moment would be though, as that was the only certainty in his recent life.

9: THE CATHOLIC LABOR PARTY

Nicola was lying in bed, awake, as he did most mornings. The breeze brought in the familiar smells of Rome and his bed was rife with filth and prepubescence. He had decided that he was going to have a lazy morning. Feeling a tingle down below the belt, he forcefully woke the boys. Knowing their life depended on it, they worked him as a team to finish him off, twice. Once he had made a mess of their faces, he promptly kicked them out. He needed the room as a young cardinal was coming to his chamber for a briefing on the situation in Boston. He didn't feel the need to dress or shower, so he just lay naked in bed waiting for Samuel's arrival, still riding the high of his orgasms.

As the guard entered to remove the children, Nicola gestured him to come closer. The guard was thankful his nose was blocked because the bed was a pig sty. "It requires both to bring me to fruition. They are useless alone. Dispose of them." The guard nodded, knowing what he was about to have to do. He escorted the children into the hallway and closed the door behind him. "There is a shortcut children. Follow me" He told them. The guard, Francesco, did not enjoy these types of activities but his families lives depended on his swift completion of the tasks the Pope assigned. As they turned a corner, their path was blocked by a dead end. Francesco quickly unsheathed his sword and leveled it at their backs. The boys slowly turned around, silently confronting their fates. He whispered "I'm so sorry" before running his blade through one boy's abdomen and completing the attack by nearly beheading the other. Their small bodies dropped into a heap of blood and flesh on the cold stone floor. He allowed a single tear to stream down his check as he watched the light in their eyes fade. He wiped the blade before sheathing it. He took a deep breath before pressing the hidden switch on the wall opening the trap door. Francesco watched their bodies tumble down into the darkness among the countless other remains in the pit. Standing at the edge of the abyss, Francesco saw his own children's faces flash before his eyes and in a split-second decision, he stepped into the pit himself, so he would never have to carry out these tasks again or have to stand in judgement by his children. The light of the opening continued to grow smaller until he felt his body hit and in a split second, everything was dark.

Once the room was clear, Nicola had a moment of reflection while lying in his filth. He remembered when he was a boy and the love he had been given by his father. He was not born into the church but rather was given to the church after a series of unfortunate family issues. The long nights of him and his father making love in his room brought warm memories and got him a little hard. His love of everything sexual was born here. The love started long before he was able to get an erection, but he felt blessed when puberty struck, and he was able to return the favors to his father. This carried on for many years until one night his sister had walked in on them. Her reaction was cross. He didn't understand why she was so upset. Father tied her up and put her in the closet, so they could finish their love making. They left her in there overnight disposed of her the next morning. Father explained that people wouldn't understand so she had to be silenced and it had to stay a family matter. Slung over father's shoulder, they brought her out into the woods behind the house. They shared her young body until she was bloody and near death. Nicola was inside of her ass from behind when father presented him with a rock. Not wanting to disappoint father, he caved in the back her skull but continued to hump until he filled her ass with his seed. They crudely buried her body in a shallow grave and returned home to continue making love to each other. A year or so after the disappearance of his sister, his father was murdered in a local pub fight. The town had their suspicions and a man much bigger than father started a drunken brawl. Nicola's mother soon became a zombie having lost so much and being in the town spotlight. He began to make love to her in absence of his father. His urges hadn't gone away, and she would not stop him. She tried at first, but she couldn't and soon just let him. One day after class, he returned home to find his mother hanging from the ceiling fan. He cut her body down and filled her uterus with his young seed once more while she was still warm. He was placed into the care of the church soon after having no family willing to house him based on the rumors. He excelled in the care of the church though, quickly rising through the ranks to his current position as Pope.

It was around the time he was placed in the care of the church that he had his first encounter with an angel. They were very nice and filled him with praise and told him how powerful he'd become as an adult. He already knew this of course, but it was nice to hear from someone else. They began coming to him frequently and helped guide his life toward his nomination for Pope. His life as Pope was amazing. He was now allowed anything he desired. He met with Poyel every month, who was much scarier than the others who came to him, but it was a necessary sacrifice for the life he now lived. No orifices were safe if he desired. Boy. Girl. Man. Woman. It mattered not. He could and would have anything he desired. Even the occasional animal would help bring him to empty his balls.

A bang at the door brought him back to reality. He had a raging erection from his daydream which he just let be. "Come in" He yelled. The door cracked open and Samuel stalked into sight. "Samuel. Come here my son." Samuel bowed and replied "Yes, heavenly father." He slowly shuffled to the bedside. "What was it you needed to tell me your holiness?" Samuel asked. "Why are you in such a rush my son? Don't you see I've an issue here in need of attending to? Are you not in need of receiving your penance? Yes?" He gestured to his erection. "As my holy father commands" Samuel said before he put the foul-smelling erection in his mouth. "That he…does" Nicola moaned.

This continued for a few minutes before Nicola instructed Samuel to disrobe and get onto the bed. "It is time for your penance my son." He told Samuel as he pointed to the bed directly in front of him. Samuel did as instructed and bent over in front of the Pope. Nicola slid his cock into Samuel's ass and began to frantically hump. Samuel lay there, dead inside, praying to whatever god that lets this happen, to just take him. Samuel also got hard and began to stroke himself. If God was watching this and letting it happen then he couldn't be mad about Samuel making the most of it. He came right before the Pope did, thankful he was able to. "Now go clean yourself up" Nicola barked at Samuel. Thankful for the dismissal, Samuel ran into the bathroom. He sat on the toilet to make sure all of Nicola's seed was gone from his body before a quick rinse in the shower. He walked back into the room and saw Nicola laying on his back, inserting a toy into his ass. "Would you like some assistance Heavenly father?" He asked, startling the Pope and making the toy become fully inserted. Nicola cried out in pain and looked angrily over at Samuel. "No. Your usefulness of the flesh has been fulfilled. Robe and listen to what I must tell you.

Samuel took a few moments to get his robes back on. He watched Nicola roll his slimy, sweaty body off the bed and did well to hide his disgust. Nicola passed Samuel on the way to the bathroom and he had to concentrate hard not to vomit as the smell hit his nostrils. The Pope came out from the bathroom after a few moments with his robes on and beckoned Samuel to sit with him near the window. "Listen my son" Nicola started saying. "I want you to go to Boston to oversee the operations there. We've word of an impending breach and I want nothing to be destroyed or taken. You've been one of my most trusted colleagues which is why I'm sending you." Samuel listened intently and nodded. "What have we done with security over there?" Samuel asked. "I've had the guards doubled and you'll be taking some of our... pets... with you." Samuel shuddered. "Very well father. When do I leave?" "You leave at once my son. Don't disappoint me or else your penance will be sevenfold next time we meet."

Samuel stood and bowed before turning toward the door and making his way quickly toward it. He knocked on the door as was customary, but no one opened it from the other side. He knocked again to the same result. Confused, he turned to look at Nicola who screamed "Open it yourself and leave me!" He did as he was told and was finally safe from any other abuse that might have come his way. The hallway outside the chamber was empty. "How odd" he thought. There was always a guard posted here. "Oh well, not my problem" he mumbled to himself as he started for his chambers to begin packing. He was not happy to be leaving the capitol, he dreaded travelling. He knew how dangerous the world was and would rather be safe from harm in these walls then exposed to the horrors of the outside world. He shuddered when he remembered he was to bring demons with him too. Nasty, filthy horrors. The stories of their escape during travel circulate from time to time and just added to his anxiety about the trip.

With his bag fully packed, Samuel made his way to the demon breeding ground beneath the Sistine Chapel. Luckily, a team of specialists handled the dirty work of creating and wrangling the beasts but going into the catacomb to reach them still made him uneasy. It wasn't too long ago a demon slipped the wranglers and eviscerated a poor priest in the tunnel. Samuel shuddered as the elevator stopped and the doors opened. He could hear their squealing but was unable to determine how far away they were because of the echo. He nearly sprinted to the office which was under a spell of protection they could not cross. Once inside, he slammed the door shut and attempted to catch his breath. The attendant inside laughed at him. "All of you are the same. Soft." He stopped laughing and with a death stare asked "What's your name? I most likely have your order ready." After a deep breath, Samuel answered. "Samuel. I'm for a special order from the top." The death stare turned into a grin once more "ooooooooh, yes. You've got a big order. Right this way young fella." He waved a hand for Samuel to follow him. Reluctantly, he made his way behind the attendant into a backroom where there was a stack of twenty or more tiny boxes on a table. "All yours Samuel. Be easy with your carry-on lad, you'll rue the day you disturb this many creatures on a plane." The attendant laughed. Samuel gulped.

10: WHY THE VATICAN WILL COLLAPSE

Ronan woke up to Taylor's beautiful face as he had every morning for the past few weeks. He watched her sleep peacefully until she stirred awake. Emma came by the room and whispered that Charles had called a meeting at command and he had requested the kids attend. Ronan rubbed a hand over her shoulder blade and down her back. She giggled from the tickle and woke up. "Charles has called for us. I think it's time for the mission they've been talking about." He was excited. "Well let's get up and over there!" Taylor said. As if he had been waiting for her to say it, he pounced out of bed. "Still can't believe these powers." He told her as he stood from the crouch he landed in. "Me either" She said as she got out of bed. He watched her intently as she walked toward him, and her breasts were bouncing. "Damn girl, why did I wait so long to make a move?" She giggled "Because we were young and thought it was the best way to protect what we had. Turns out what we had was this all along." She came right up to him and gave him a sensual kiss on the lips before stalking into the bathroom. "Get ready" she called. "Let's go see what we've got waiting for us."

After the kids had gotten ready, they met Emma and Henrik in the living room and traveled to the pyramid together. They had never seen the building so full of people. Whatever was happening was very important. Charles and Shakir were talking with Victor near what looked like a large 3d map of something. A team of people in riot gear were huddled with Attila near an open weapons cache close by. Dad pointed out "The Thule's elite strike team has assembled." Ronan noticed Al was one of them. His hulking body stood out among the crowd. Ronan walked over to talk to him. "I didn't know you were on the strike team" he said to Al. With a welcoming smile, he responded "Vitae is my blood. I've got a certain... usefulness" he chuckled "On the battle field." Ronan laughed with him. "We'll talk in a bit young master." He pat Ronan on the back before returning his attention to Attila. Ronan met back up with his family just as Charles noticed they had arrived. "Corvers!" He called loudly. The room's attention turned toward them. "Good morning to you all. I'm glad to see you're suited up and ready." Charles walked closer to continue the conversation. The room goes back about its business. "Go see Attila to get outfitted with weapons and we'll begin the briefing." He directed at the kids. Emma told them "We'll be around you guys. Pay attention, this will be your first mission." She seemed excited about it. Henrik said "I'm proud of you guys. You've been doing well from what I hear." "Thanks" Ronan said back. "We're doing our best." Taylor nodded. "We're pushing hard to get up to speed." "Well get to it" Emma pointed to the SWAT group and smiled.

Ronan and Taylor hugged Emma before marching over and joining the huddle. "Ronan, Taylor, this is Adam." Attila pointed to the man next to him. "You'll be riding with his team." "Good to finally meet you two. We've heard great things" Adam said to them. Ronan noticed his faint German accent, but he hid it well. "After the briefing, we're going to run some drills, you two will join us" He directed. "Sounds good to us" Ronan replied. Charles called attention to the full group gathered. "Please take your seats everyone. We're going to get started in a moment." The huddle began to file onto some benches near where Charles and Shakir were standing. "Follow me quickly" Attila said to the kids. He reached into the open weapon cache and pulled out two weapons. "You'll need these for the training exercises and the mission. Take them with you." He handed one to each kid. "Now go sit with the team and pay good attention." Two seats had been saved for them. Charles began talking as they sat. "Our next step in disrupting enemy activity is to abduct a cardinal who will be visiting from Rome." Shakir started next. "He'll know how to get us the Pope." Ronan stood and asked, "What is the plan once we have the Pope?" The SWAT team looked at Ronan in shock. Charles smiled and answered, "We really haven't gotten that far yet. We've been focused on building a force and less on what we're going to use it for." He seemed sincere. "Well do we know where the enemy's headquarters are located?" Ronan asked. Shakir answered "Not a clue." Victor stood "The same cloaking device that keeps us hidden also keeps their base a secret to us." Ronan is connecting the dots. "So, don't we think the Pope will know how to find the base?" Charles replied, "It's a solid bet he'll know how to find it." Ronan jumps into a fighting stance "So I say we get this guy, nab the Pope, and squeeze him to tell us where to find the base. Once we find it, we destroy it. Once and for all." Adam and his team stand and cheer in agreement. "I like how this guy thinks" Adam shouted. "I mean, that's as solid a plan as any we've come up with to this point. It will eventually lead to something of the sort, so what the hell. Sounds like we've got a roadmap. Let's save the planet. Thank you, Mr. Corvers." The team cheered again before settling down. They started paying attention again as Charles began.

"So, step one of the plan involves getting our hands on this cardinal. Sources tell us he'll be arriving tonight from Rome. He's going to be hold up in the Boston Archdiocese. They're a pompous bunch so we shouldn't meet too much resistance." Shakir stepped up. "We'll be sending two teams in for a quick extraction. Team one will land ground level as a diversionary tactic. Team two will drop on the roof and breach from there. Like Charles said, we don't expect much resistance but as you all know, we don't under prepare. The goal of this mission is to get the cardinal extracted by whatever means necessary. If anyone or anything" He smiled, "gets in the way of the mission, take it out." The word *anything* brought Ronan back to the Reis' basement and that demon attack. He was sure this is what Shakir meant. He was kind of hoping one would be there now that he had the weapons and training, so he could dispatch it himself. "Your leaders have your orders. You know the mission. Get into the simulator and run through the motions a few times until you think you're good." Shakir finished the briefing. Adam stood and nodded. "Team. You heard him." The team stood and cleanly filed through a far door. Adam walked over to the kids. "I see you've got your weapons. Join us in the simulator." He told them. Attila was ruffling in the weapons cache. "Ronan. Taylor. One more thing" Attila called out. Adam gestured them to go see Attila before following the team into the door. "Load up with these side weapons." He handed each of them a pistol. "This is your first simulation. We're all anxious to see how you two do."

Armed up and amped, the kids walked through the doors. On the other side, they entered onto a platform with a couple mean looking helicopters. Beyond the dock, there was a vast expanse of nature. "Wow, they've got amazing simulators down here. That looks real." Taylor whispered to Ronan. He was impressed as well. Adam called from inside one of the choppers "Hop inside guys. We're moving out." The kids got onboard and harnessed in. The chopper smoothly lifted off of the ground and moved toward the opening. Taylor made eye contact with Ronan. She was nervous. He smiled at her to hopefully reassure her but instead, his stomach dropped as the chopper began to dive straight down. He could see the water fast approaching and began to worry himself. He looked to the rest of the team to try and gauge their reactions. No one else seemed worried so he took a deep breath. The back of the chopper began to level, and it started moving forward very quickly, skimming the water. The other chopper pulled up beside theirs. Ronan could see Shakir standing inside the other vehicle. Adam screamed so the team could hear "We're approaching the drop point. Lock and load." Ronan pulled his charging handle back like he had learned in training, made sure the barrel was free of obstructions, and let it forward again. He was ready for whatever was coming. The team began to unsnap their harness buckles, so he did the same and saw Taylor following suit. The chopper dropped toward the ground and they rushed out with the rest of the team into the unknown.

His stomach dropped as he stepped off the side of the chopper and began to fall. They were much higher than he initially thought, and panic struck him. He calmed his mind like Shakir had been teaching him and he saw clarity in the situation. Everyone else was falling as well. They wouldn't commit suicide for a training exercise. Everything was fine. He took a deep breath and braced himself for the impact about to happen.

His landing was surprisingly soft. "This vitae is insane" He thought to himself, still not fully knowing the extent of his new abilities. A cloud of dust was beginning to form as the choppers hovered while more of the team dropped onto the ground near him. His visibility of the surrounding area was deteriorating. He could see the team blocking up though, so he quickly joined the other members as a blood curdling scream pierced his ears. Weapon ready, he kept his back pressed against the person behind him as they moved in formation. "Be ready" Adam quietly warned. Worried about Taylor, he quickly looked to the group and was relieved to see some of her hair showing from under her helmet. While looking forward at her, he noticed an extremely large shadow rising up in the dust cloud in front of the group.

Ronan followed the immense shadow with his eyes until it had reached its full height. He watched the maw slowly open before a near deafening roar rocked the ground they stood on. The rest of the team finally noticed the creature and dropped into firing position. Following suit, Ronan kneeled and opened fire instantly as the command came from Adam's mouth. The creature was so large that it seemed it was moving in slow motion as it reacted to the gunfire. It dropped back onto four legs with a loud thud before launching one of its front claws toward the group. "INCOMING" one of the team yelled out. Ronan stood and pushed off hard to avoid the attack, launching himself at least twenty feet into the air. He watched the claw dragging on the ground as it moved, leaving a mess of torn up earth in its wake. Ronan landed in the small canyon left behind by the creature. He noticed the team was scattered but still firing on the massive beast, so he continued firing as well. Aiming for the usual soft spots, he unloaded his clip as he had been taught. The dust cloud made it impossible to tell if the creature was wounded but he continued to fire until he heard otherwise.

Carefully moving closer to the beast, he had an epiphany. Pulling his headset over his eyes, he switched on his heat vision hoping for a better view of the battle. Only a few team members became visible and he panicked. Practicing his breathing, he was able to relax long enough to think back to his time studying with Victor. Some residents of Hyperborea were undead. They wouldn't show up on heat scans. This reassured him about his headset not showing the whole team, but the creature wasn't showing up either which didn't help his anxiety. Keeping the goggles on his face for a moment longer, he rescanned the area again, looking for anything that he might have missed. About to remove the goggles and rejoin the fray, he noticed a heat blip floating in the air off in the distance. Utilizing the zoom feature, he took a closer look. It was a body curled into the fetal position. He could see that something wasn't quite right though. It had multiple growths coming off of it and it was shaking around as if it was moving. "How can that be?" He thought to himself.

A loud thud shook the ground he stood on and he quickly removed his goggles. The beast was unsettlingly close to him. He pulled the goggles back down and then up again, working the situation out in his head. The body was inside of the beast! It finally clicked. He thought back to Lisa and the demon who had infected her. Victor had taught them that demons are just parasites who infect hosts. The body he saw must be the host which means this thing is a demon. Gunfire and shouting in the distance sucked him back to the battle. Locking his headset in the up position, he aimed his rifle forward and fired as he began to charge forward. He needed to find Taylor to let her know what he had figured out. He knew how to bring the beast down.

After finding an alcove to take cover in, he brought his wrist close to his face. "Quinn" He called into his wrist, "Hone in on my location, I've got a plan." "Copy" she replied. He felt a great deal of relief knowing she was ok. Staying prone, he moved up to get a look at the scene. A small group of soldiers was full sprinting forward at him. The reason why soon became evident as the tail of the beast became visible through the dust, moving very quickly behind them. Ronan rolled sideways so they could jump in the hole to safety. Protecting his face, he felt the other team members hit the bottom of the hole as they slid in to safety. Not even a moment later, the tail of the beast slid over the top of the crater throwing rock and dust onto the team in hiding.

"This thing is massive!" Taylor commented as she wiped herself off. Ronan's face lit up. "There you are. So, check this out." He said to the group. "This thing is a demon. Remember how I told you the demon who attacked me in the Reis' basement was Lisa?" He asked Taylor. "Of course, I do. I still have nightmares about it." She replied. "Well, Victor has been teaching us how demons are leeches, right? This thing has a body inside of it. I saw it." He said pointing to his goggles. "I'm picking up what you're putting down." Taylor told him. "You two" Ronan directed at the other team members, "reconnect with the team and call the extraction. There's about to be a big bang." The man on the right jumped up and gave a hand to the other. Once both stood, he spoke the kids. "I'll get everyone rounded up. What're you going to do?" Taylor looked at Ronan before answering. "Kill its host."

The duo locked and loaded their weapons before sprinting out of the crater. Ronan and Taylor did the same in the opposite direction but silently, hoping the creature would be distracted enough to let them get close. Skillfully navigating underneath the creature, Ronan dropped his heat goggles to pinpoint where the host was above them. Taylor removed the hunnish blade just as Attila had instructed them and readied her strike. Ronan gave the word once they had arrived directly beneath the body. "We're not going to get much time to get this done once we start" Ronan reminded her. She nodded. "I'm going to open it wide enough for both of us. Will need help finding my way out." He wrapped his left arm around her back and locked his goggles up with his other hand before kissing her lips. "It's all yours, girl. Get it." He moved back and readied his sword as well. Taylor crouched in attack position before pushing off hard, sword readied to strike. As she got in range of the creature's stomach, she swiftly dragged the blade forward opening a rather large wound which immediately began to seep black ooze. Ronan watched her return to the ground and land perfectly. He wished Attila could have seen it, she executed it perfectly. With his sword drawn, he joined her and together, they pushed off hard and entered the newly opened wound.

Darkness engulfed the two as the wound quickly sealed behind them. Ronan reached out and grabbed Taylor's hand. She squeezed letting him know she was ok. Trying to take in the surroundings, he noticed random flashes of light bouncing off the shiny walls. "See that?" He asked her. "Yea, I do. You think that's the body? Let's go look anyway, this smell is going to kill me." They laughed as they trudged forward toward the sporadic light flashes. Ronan walked into a gooey wall which was blocking their path forward. It seemed like the light was coming from behind the wall though, so he felt around and found a crack he could squeeze through. "If I'm not back in twenty minutes, send a search party" He told her, secretly grinning because of the darkness. "I'm coming right behind you, ya turd." She replied with a laugh. Holding his breath, he squeezed his body through the crack and found himself in an open space and was blinded. It took a moment for his eyes to adjust but once they had started, he was able to see well enough to grab

Taylor's hand and help her through. While she was adjusting her eyes, he scanned the room for the source of the light. Floating in the middle of the room, a naked male body was pulsating with light. The body was pierced by multiple spikes that held it in suspension. "Whelp" He started, "That's it." She gave her eyes a final rub and viewed the scene for herself. "Ya know, a few months ago something like would've ruined me." They laughed. "You ready to move?" She asked. He nodded as he drew his blade. "Hit it babe" He replied. She drew her blade and expertly sliced through the spikes holding the body while exposing the head. One final clean sweep and the head was separated from the shoulders, bouncing as it hit the floor. The larger creature started writhing, throwing them around. "Time to go my love. I'm thinking straight up." Ronan told her, pointing to the celling with his blade. She nodded and stepped back. He pulled his sword back into attack stance, and with a forceful forward strike, opened a wound in the top of the creature. "Go!" He yelled as the creature began to wildly shake. "I'm right behind you." He called out. He watched Taylor jump through the wound to safety and he swiftly followed.

The situation hadn't drastically improved on the outside of the creature. The creatures writhing was creating a bigger dust storm and its body had started to pulsate with light. Ronan knew what was coming and his nerves were on edge. The wrist communicator started to buzz, and Adam came through the speaker. "Ronan!" He called out. "Do you copy?" He answered into the device "Adam, we're on the creatures back. We've neutralized it so hurry the hell up and get us away from here." Taylor wrapped her arms around Ronan and squeezed. "Choppers inbound. 10 seconds." Adam called through. He looked down at Taylor "Nice job by the way babe. You're a fuckin' badass." Her rosy cheeks were visible even through the dust. The cloud began to dissipate as the chopper dropped from the sky above nearing where they were standing. A hand reached out from the cabin and Ronan put Taylor forward to meet it. Once she was safely onboard, he jumped into the cabin beside her. Adam was inside, brandishing a huge smile. "Get us out of here" he yelled to the pilot. The kids strapped in as the chopper began moving hastily away from the scene. "Paying attention in class I see?" Adam directed at the kids. "Of course, we are." Ronan replied. "I'll never be caught defenseless again. I'll never let her either." Adam looked impressed. "Good man. Well you both passed the test. Our orders were to let you two at it. Support if needed but stand by. I've got a very promising report to deliver upon our return." Ronan and Taylor fist bumped in excitement. "So, you guys didn't do anything?" Taylor asked with a smile on her face. "Nope" Adam replied. "Just pissed it off. Couldn't make it easy for you" He smiled. "You should've seen Maynard's test" pointing to a member of the team. The entire chopper erupted in laughter. "A story for another time." He finished.

The eruption of the blast sounded off below them and shook the chopper slightly. Ronan was happy to have been so far away from this explosion remembering the one at the Reis' house. "And there it is." Adam commented. The group began to applaud. "Welcome to the team."

11: PRIESTS AND DEMONS

The serene atmosphere never helped the morning routine feel any better. He had hoped it might someday since he enjoyed it so much. The archdiocese site was close enough to the ocean to enjoy the cool breeze from the coastal winds but too far to enjoy the sands. The smell of rose bushes blooming in the yard mixed with coffee blew into the young man's path as he followed his mentor outside. Many young priests were out walking the loop as was the case most mornings. They would come outside nearly every morning to talk with their mentors before morning mass. Samuel watched from his bedroom window, reliving those morning walks. He had slept terribly the night before and felt it this morning. His sleeplessness wasn't caused by the worry he'd normally have of being violated, like these young men were about to experience, but rather he had laid awake because the demons could be heard pacing the hallway outside his room and the terrible noises they produced echoed throughout his bed chamber. Unimaginable noises came out of these things which produced pictures in his head reminiscent of maggots being squished, flesh tearing, and newborns crying. He would need more than a few cups of the coffee this morning to get his head right for the day ahead. "At least the sunlight will keep the creatures in the shadows" he thought to himself. He felt safe for the time being.

The young man who had been following his mentor stopped for a moment and let the breeze caress his face. He had convinced himself that the beauty of nature he experienced each morning was the only positive thing in his day, so he tried to enjoy it for as long as he could. "Come boy" His mentor shouted. "This sacrament isn't going to fix itself." The boy silently exhaled, knowing full well what was to come, and began to follow again. The men walked toward the secluded east side of the property. "Closest to the ocean" he thought, trying to keep his thoughts positive. They had ventured quite far from the building and found a bench to rest on while discussing whatever "religious" business they were to go over this day. The mentor reached into the young man's robe and began to stroke his inner thighs, like he did most mornings. The boy closed his eyes and sank into himself as he had gotten used to doing during these times. The older man's hand reached and wrapped around his shaft and it began to grow. His eyes being closed, he only heard the old man disrobing in his ears before a noise that sounded like a melon being squished. He snapped back to reality, though it took him a moment to come out of his daze. The feeling of a warm liquid on his face and prompted him to run a finger across his forehead to see what it was. Bringing his hand into eyesight, the blood on it didn't register as a problem because he saw through his fingers and his mentor on the ground; pants around his ankles, dick hard, with a gaping hole in his forehead.

The young man sat frozen for a moment, warm blood running down his face. A faint buzzing could be heard on the horizon so wasting no time, he stood and started sprinting toward the building. "JOSIAH IS DEAD" He began to shout as he ran. "HE'S DEAD". He opened his mouth to shout again as a shooting pain hit the back of his neck and an explosion of blood and teeth shot out of his mouth. An unbearable pain plagued him for a split second before he dropped dead to the ground. A few groups of people closer to the building had heard someone shouting and now noticed the faint buzzing sound growing louder by the second. "What's that noise father?" Another young boy asked his mentor. Before he could come up with a good answer, two helicopters appeared on the horizon and began rapidly firing on the building. The priests jumped for cover, using their mentees as human shields, while bullets ripped through the yard and open balconies. One chopper landed in the courtyard among the bodies of the religious. The passengers kept suppressing fire on the building while the other landed on the roof.

Samuel, sitting in the rectory, enjoying his coffee and the peace of the morning, thought he heard someone screaming in the distance. He couldn't tell if it was his brain playing tricks on him, but his question was answered when he heard the gunfire rip against the side of building. He was startled and spilled his coffee on his lap. "Fuck" he cursed under his breath as he stood to clean his lap. Another round of gunfire pelted the outside wall and he jumped for cover. Once it had passed, he began the journey back to his office for an update as to what the hell that was. The papal security intercepted him in route and joined him. "We must hurry to the safe room" one of the guards said to Samuel. "I need the book I brought from Rome. The enemy mustn't get a hold of it." He replied. "Quickly then" The guard spoke to the team. They moved with haste through the halls toward the office as mayhem unfolded around them. The gunfire was loud, people were screaming, and he could hear the demons in the shadows. Samuel thought to himself "I need to get out of this life before I have a stroke." They reached the office door just as an explosion ripped through the building above them.

The papal security push Samuel into the office and seem double in number as they all enter. A radio on the shoulder of one of the guards screams out "They've breached the roof access and are coming in." and violently ended with gunfire. "We need to move. Now." Another of the guards in the room called out as he reloaded his rifle. "Is your business here done?" He asked Samuel. Not yet getting the book, he scrambled to the desk and got his hands on it. "Yes" he promptly responded. The guards grouped around Samuel and began to move toward the safety of the basement. Samuel noticed the security guards flipping the UV spotlights active on their weapons as one of them called into the radio "Cut the shades!" A loud mechanical noise rang through the building and with multiple loud bangs, window by window, metal shades began to slam down over the openings. Samuel started to get nervous because he could hear the demons in the shadows. They were getting louder as if they were cheering. The guards tightened the circle to make sure the UV covered them all as they crept through the halls in what was soon complete darkness. Samuel had little comfort though because he had seen a demon in action many times before and it was something he'd hoped he'd never have to see again.

As the final cover closed, the demons swarmed from the shadows. They moved around the group because of the UVs but the humans weren't spared the terror. The smell was reminiscent of rotten garbage and enough of the monstrosities could be seen to disrupt a sleep pattern. Thankfully, Samuel thought, they left the main building and the corridor they entered was demon free. It seemed like they'd be reaching their destination soon judging by the number of stairs they had descended. They turned a corner and came upon a large metal door which the group stopped in front of. Two of the men began working on opening it. Samuel was anxious to get inside to safety. They hadn't seen a demon for a good while, but the battle could be heard none the less. A great flash of light shined from the direction they had come from and in this moment, Samuel noticed the mayhem had died down. The building was nearly silent save the men opening the door. They finally were able to nudge the door open and one of them turned to guide Samuel inside when his right eye exploded out in a burst of red and he fell to the ground. Samuel quickly looked around at the others as they all began to fall. Nearly instantly, he found himself standing in the middle of a pile of bodies, covered in blood and alone. A group of men with their rifles trained on him appeared out of the darkness.

One of them grabbed him by the arm and threw him of off his feet into the room. The rest of the group followed him into the room and barred the door after closing it. They dropped their weapons and one of them took his facemask off. Samuel had a very odd feeling he'd seen this man's face somewhere before but couldn't place it. "Good morning Cardinal" The man said to him, heavy sarcasm laced his voice. "I hope you don't mind that we've joined you in this little retreat. It seems to be the safest place in this joint. Did you see those demons out there?" He asked with a giant smirk on his face.

12: CHANGE OF WORLD VIEW

The time had finally come. Mission day. Ronan was too excited to sleep long. He woke up before Taylor but let her sleep until she started to stir. "We should get ready" He whispered to her. She giggled. "Did you sleep at all?" She asked. "Too excited" He replied. "Well let's get up" She offered. He waited to watch her sit up to get a view of her breasts as the covers fell off of them. No matter the occasion he made time for the little things. After a quick shower, they grabbed the gear that they'd gathered the night before and headed for the pyramid. It was early, but the entire group had already shown up by the time they had arrived. Ronan found his way to the weapons table, but Taylor didn't immediately follow because the spectacle of the whole operation prep had her in a daze. It looked like something out of a movie and even after all she'd seen, this caught her attention hard. "Hey Taylor!" Ronan called to her. "Come get your weapon set up". She snapped back to reality and wandered over to the station where he was beginning to build his rifle. She noticed Ronan watching her as she started hers but knew he only wanted to help if she needed it. She was reminded for a moment why she loved him. Speeding through her routine, she surprised him and finished her last modification before he did. "Let's go slow poke" she smirked at him. He snapped his buttstock down and grabbed her behind her head to pull her in for a kiss. He let her go and looked her in the eyes. "Stay close to me today and let's make this a success." She blushed "Ok." She said. "We did really well as a team yesterday plus I'm looking to get a few demons back for what they did to you!" He laughed. "Looks like they're gathering near the choppers, let's go!" They joined the group as Charles began to address the crowd.

"We've beaten this to death. You each know what is expected of you. Extract the Cardinal and anything important he may have brought from Rome. This war is coming to a head. Today's successful mission brings us closer to the next phase. Don't let us down. The world itself depends on it." The group stood and cheered. One the crowd settled down, they began to head for the choppers. Adam checked in with the kids before boarding. "You two did very well yesterday. How're you feeling about today? Are you ready?" Taylor answered for the, both "Hell yea we're ready!" Adam and Ronan laughed. "We're going to keep together and help the team" Ronan said. Adam nodded. "Good plan. Let's get this thing started."

Two choppers held a handful of men and women. Adam boarded the other chopper while Shakir was in the chopper with the kids. The engines roared to life and the two birds lifted off. Shakir stood and addressed the team. "Everyone strapped in?" He asked. Ronan checked on Taylor's harness. She smiled big. Ronin nodded to him after quickly checking his own. Shakir smirked, sat down, and strapped himself moments before the chopper dropped off the side of the platform.

Ronan hadn't really explored outside of the city and wasn't sure about the tunnels around it but was curious how they planned on getting these birds topside. He was sure that the pilots knew what they were doing but a small inkling of fear was sitting in his gut. He'd never seen the bottom side of the city either and it was a site to behold as they flew away from it. The city sat on a giant platform held up by a single pole structure in the middle. Below them was a giant lake which the pole holding the city disappeared into. The space was immense but, on the outskirts, they were surrounded by dirt walls as one would expect being underground. The choppers began to level out and fly straight toward one of these walls. Taylor started to squeeze his hand, echoing his own concern. He looked over to Shakir and saw he was brandishing that damn smirk he always had. He winked at Ronan which prompted him to take a deep breath and stop worrying. Ronan rubbed Taylor's hand and yelled into her ear "Watch. Somethings about to happen." He knew it was going to be fine, but the buildup was intense because they were moments away from crashing into the wall. Seconds before impact, Ronan watched as a massive hole began to dig itself into the side of the dirt wall. The whole grew to a massive size and they flew right into it as it closed behind them. Spotlights flashed on and illuminated their surroundings. From what he could see, the tunnel seemed to be digging itself around them. Shakir yelled "The Lemurians have some amazing earth bending tech. We'll be there in no time." Ronan had told himself almost daily he'd stop being shocked by things but here he sat, mind completely blown.

An hour or so had passed since flying into the wall. Shakir stood and shouted "Get your masks on. The sunlight will kill your eyes or just kill you in general. Maynard, I mean you" The group laughed. Ronan laughed to himself, just getting the joke. "Guess vampires really can't do sunlight." He looked over at Taylor who pointed between her legs and Ronan remembered seeing the masks attached to the chair. He grabbed his and placed it over his head. His field of vision became filled with floating green diagnostics of the world around him. He noticed the heart rate of a guy sitting adjacent from him as well as an outline of his skeletal structure. "These things are amazing" He yells to Taylor who's looking around in hers too. The momentum of the chopper changes which dropped his stomach. "We're rising" She yells to him. Before he can reply, above them opens in a beam of light and water rushes in around them. They slowly rose out of the ocean into the sky. Ronan looked down to where they'd just come from and watched the hole seal itself as ocean water rushed back in. Moments later, it looked like it had never opened in the first place.

They continued to rise and without warning, lurched forward at a very fast speed. The man sitting nearest the door unbuckled himself and opened the door. He attached a strap to his belt buckle and the side of the seat before sitting on the edge. He opened a gun case and began to assemble a rifle with a long barrel and a large scope. "Sniper" Ronan yelled to Taylor. Shakir stood and addressed the group. "Almost go time. Unharness. Safeties off. Feuer Frei!" He smiled. The group shouted in unison "Bang, Bang" while hitting their chests on beat. Ronan couldn't help but smile. As if his new life wasn't exciting enough, they were also Rammstein fans. He made a mental note to talk to Shakir about that later.

Soon, the ocean gave way to the harbor and they crossed onto land keeping their current pace. Ronan watched as the sniper picked up his rifle and began to dial in the scope. "We're touching down on the roof and Adam's team is landing in the yard to offer a diversion." Shakir yelled, reminding the team. "As soon as we hit the roof, dismount and get to cover. The ground team will keep them busy while we breach the roof access. That's your team Maynard. Once inside, clear any resistance in our way and get the Cardinal, alive. Questions?" The group grunted in acknowledgment. They had just drilled the day before and all felt confident in the plan.

The sniper chambered a round very smoothly, as if it was his millionth time doing so, and let off a shot. He reloaded and sent another, all within the span of about 5 seconds. He stood after the shots and bowed to hoots and hollers from the team, setting the rifle on a rack before taking his seat and grabbing his semi auto. The chopper slowed, and the team stood, ready to move. Ronan made sure Taylor was up and she had her gun. She smiled behind her mask but knew she was ready. The time had finally come. They watched Adam's chopper drop into the courtyard, firing on the building, as theirs headed for the roof. As soon as they felt it hit the building, they moved out onto the roof as a group and set up their perimeter very fluidly. The gunfire below was echoing around them, but no resistance could be seen from the church yet. Two of the guys moved on the roof access. "Maynard" Ronan thought. He watched as they circled the hatch, setting charges. The haste of their retreat affirmed that's what they had just done. A few seconds later, a rather large explosion ripped through the door and took a good portion of the roof with it. Shakir stood from his crouch and yelled "Ok! move in, they were bound to hear that!" The team moved into a stacked formation and proceeded through the newly formed gash in the roof. The team leader stopped moving and quietly said "The office is this way" He pointed to the left "but I studied the plans yesterday and I have a pretty good idea of where they'll be going and it's not the office." Shakir responded. "We're following you. You're leading this for a reason" With a nod, he began to move the team toward the right, slowly descending into the building. Ronan was clearing corners and hallways just like they had trained. He looked to Taylor briefly in his scanning and was happy to see her doing the same. He worried for her but not because she wasn't capable. She had kicked his ass plenty of times. As they approached the base of the stairs, a near constant gunfire could be heard and he snapped back to focus. The group emerged from the staircase and met Adam's team, who was battling a demon horde. The scene was like that out of a nightmare. Adams team was surrounded by a shield of UV and waves of demons were descending upon them.

Ronan yelled to Taylor "The one I dealt with was pretty terrible and there are so many more here." She could sense panic in his voice. She blew him a kiss but couldn't help but feel slightly worried too. Adam yelled to them while firing. "Follow tight along the east wall. We saw them headed that way. He's with them. We'll take care of these disgusting things." While he was talking, a demon crawled out from the horde and entered the UV circle. It stood on its hind legs showing an underside covered in hundreds of tiny razor-sharp feet. Adam turned to face the demon. The UV was hurting the demon because smoke started rising from its body but all it did was let out a blood curdling scream before it lunged at Adam. He calmly side stepped out of its trajectory and beheaded the creature with a single swing of his serrated sword. Ronan didn't even see him unsheathe it. Adam slid the sword back into the sheath and gave the body a heavy kick out of the UV. Shakir acted as if nothing had just happened and yelled over the gunfire "Was Maynard's plan all along. Promote him when we get back." Adam patted Maynard on the shoulder and pointed toward the route his team was opening for them. "Move out. Get them before the panic room closes. We'll never get into it if they close it and we'll lose him." The team stacked back up and began to move toward a very dark corner of the building. Maynard veered the team through a side hallway which sparked a question from Shakir. "Is this the way Adam spoke of?" He asked, skeptical though not sincere. "Told you, I studied the layout. This will bring us directly into the hallway adjacent from the path they'd have taken." Maynard replied while pointing. "Trust me" He finished before beginning to move the stack again.

This hall brought them down another set of stairs which opened to a large hallway, clearly underground. Maynard stopped the group and whispered "Night vision and low impact. They're here." Once the night vision was active, Ronan could see a group of armed men and a religious figure behind them. The cardinal he presumed. The end of the hall his group was in was completely dark and gave perfect cover. The team spread out and trained their rifles on the guards. "They are opening the door. Let them." Shakir whispered. He raises his hand and held it while the men worked on opening the door. "Each of you take one guard, from right to left. Leave the cardinal unharmed." Ronan and Taylor quickly looked to their left and right and fixed their sights on their respective church guard. Once the door cracked, Shakir dropped his hand and the team hit all of the guards nearly instantly. The cardinal was left standing. Covered in blood, alone, and in shock. Maynard quickly commanded "Move out" and the group edged toward the man with their rifles up. Ronan reached the cardinal first and grabbed him by his arm. He forcefully moved the man into the safe room and the team followed. Once the last man had entered, they barred the door. Shakir removed his mask and spoke to the cardinal. "Good morning Cardinal" He began "I hope you don't mind that we've joined you in this little retreat. It seems to be the safest place in this joint. Did you see those demons out there?" He asked with his signature smirk. Ronan was smiling under his mask.

13: THE ESCAPE

The initial mission was complete. The cardinal was in custody and the team was safe for the time being. They removed their helmets, so they could take a moment and relax. The cardinal looked cross at the situation though. "You've fallen into a trap!" He screamed. "You've got no means of escape." Shakir laughed out loud. "Well you're not going anywhere either so pipe down your *eminence*." He replied. A couple of the guys laughed. The cardinal, embarrassed, had no reply. Ronan approached Shakir and whispered to him "So what is the plan? The remaining guards will be in here soon and he's not lying. We're trapped." Shakir stood and placed his hands on Ronan's shoulders. "Don't worry. This has all been planned." He then walked toward the far wall and stopped, staring at the stones. A loud bang is heard on the other side of the door. Startled, Taylor came over to Ronan and asked him "What did he say?" He giggled "He said they've got a plan and not to worry." He shrugged his shoulders. "With all the weird crap that we've seen, this is no time to lose faith, right? I'm curious to see what's going to happen. I've got a feeling something crazy is coming." She hugged him tightly around his trunk for a good, long moment. She let go and told him "I think you're right. I hope you're right. There's only one door in or out of here and hordes of demons and armed guards are trying to get through it. I'd hope we had some sort of escape plan" Ronan could hear Shakir whispering to the wall. He can't make out any of the words except for the word "*Luciferi*."

The banging on the door intensified with time. The team began prepping for a breach. Desks were overturned for cover and rifles were trained on the door. Through all the commotion, Shakir hadn't moved from the wall. His body was so still it seemed time around him had ceased motion. A very loud, deep, noise rang through the room that caused everyone to jump and focus on the door. Ronan continued to watch Shakir though as he stepped back from the wall. The stones in front of him began to separate and restructure almost like the earth wall had opened for the chopper on their way to the surface. Once they realized what was happening, the team stacked back up behind Shakir, the cardinal in hand. Taylor joined Ronan and watched as the stones continued to separate from each other until a large hole had been formed and the rocks settled. The hole was more than big enough to comfortably fit the whole group. Not much could be seen beyond the entrance, but it looked like it continued downward. "This trek isn't over yet" Maynard broke the silence and told the group. "Masks back on. We're going underground." He pointed to Samuel. "You're still alive for a reason. Do NOT do anything to make me rethink that." Samuel looked terrified. Shakir giggled. The group formed a circle around the Cardinal and moved into the hole. Ronan was at the rear of the circle and watched the hole close behind them as they trucked into it. Darkness closed in around them and even their masks didn't seem to help illuminate their surroundings. Ronan could hear the cardinal quietly whimpering and had a moment of sympathy for the man before remembering what the church, and this man, stood for.

Having lost the Cardinal, Bishop Mike Melle oversaw the archdiocese. Once they realized the cardinal's team had been slain and he was being held inside the panic room, they scrambled all of their remaining resources to the basement to get that door open. The might of their remaining forces worked tirelessly to break that door down and save the cardinal. "They have nowhere to run" he thought. The bishop stood by for a good fifteen minutes while his team worked to remove the hinges and drop the steel door, so they could enter. Once the door was finally released from its tight hold and fell hard onto the floor, his team breached. No gunfire or shouting was heard. Mike was suspicious and pushed through the men to enter the room himself. He couldn't believe his eyes when he finally got inside. The room was completely empty. Mike's head began to pound. Regardless of where they went or how they got there, he would have to explain to the pope, personally, that even with the extra security and prior knowledge of the attack, they had lost the cardinal. His day had just got decidedly worse.

He took his time making his way back to the office. Mike ordered the shades to be pulled back up and for the mess to be cleaned on his way. The demons roared and hissed in anger as the sunlight began to permeate the halls again. Mike could feel the stress lift and how thankful the men were to banish them back to the shadows. They really were disgusting abominations though he'd grown accustomed to their filth. Moseying up toward the second floor, he finally decided to just get it over with. He knew the Holy Father would want to hear of this failure right away and delaying any further would be worse for him. He retreated into the office to make the call to Rome. He turned to close the doors and as they shut, his body started to ache because it knew how the Holy Father reacted to bad news. It knew all too well.

14: TRIALS AND TRIBULATIONS OF THE ESCAPE

The group had been walking for a few moments before Ronan noticed the tunnel opening into a large corridor. Flame torches lined the walls of this new tunnel they had just connected with. It spanned in both directions as far as anyone could see. Shakir took off his mask and pointed toward the right. "This is where we're headed." Samuel whined "how much farther are we walking?" Maynard barked "Well lucky for you, we've got a ride inbound. It's for my team though so don't think your comfort is of any concern to me." Samuel scowled. Taylor piped in breaking up the confrontation brewing "Where is this ride?" She asked. "Should be here any moment." He replied while looking at his watch.

The ground began to vibrate under their feet and a noise rang off in the distance. Both faint at first. Shakir moved back toward the wall and the team followed. Ronan grabbed Taylor and followed suit. "Who the hell knows what that is" Ronan thought. The noise and vibration grew louder and louder until a light appeared down the tunnel, getting bigger and brighter as time passed. "A train?" Ronan asked, surprised. Taylor nodded. "Looks like it." She laughed. The sheer monstrosity of the vehicle took Ronan by surprise. It was one of the meanest looking trains he'd ever seen. The engine car had a large plow on its base and two large smoke stacks. A singular red eye could be seen on the front which Ronan guessed must've been a window. Many other smaller pipes lined the sides of the cars that passed, leaking steam and protected by spikes. Ronan looked at Taylor "Just when I think I've seen it all, something crazier comes along." She responded "I was thinking the same thing. Life has been a wild ride these past couple of months and it's getting crazier by the day, still! Happy to be sharing it with you though." She pressed her lips on his and kept them there for a moment. Shakir yelled "Come on love birds, we're moving out! Make out on the train" The kids stopped kissing, giggled, and followed the group as they boarded one of the cars. Before they'd completely settled, the train began to lurch forward. The ride was unlike any he'd ever experienced before. Once it got going, he wouldn't have even known he was moving if he couldn't see objects moving outside. He finally sat next to Taylor and enjoyed the time to decompress. More was coming, he was sure of it.

Ronan watched as Taylor dozed off and he must've soon after because Shakir startled him when he sat next to them on the bench. "There are some things coming up I think you'll find… enjoyable" He told them. "I can only imagine what it will be next!" Ronan replied. Taylor laughed. "Trust me." Shakir said. "You haven't even touched the surface yet." He stood, smirked, and walked away. "Well let's get up and go look" Taylor poked. "He said it's cool." Ronan let out an extended sigh. "I'm comfy" he said before slowly getting up from the seat. Taylor was giving him a look. "You're right. Why I'm up!" He curtsied which made her laugh out loud. "Shakir's up toward the front of the train. Let's find him."

Walking past the team, the cardinal shot Ronan a dirty look, which he returned. Maynard gave Samuel a smack on the back of the head having noticed the encounter. "Trying my patience father" he said aloud. The team laughed at this and Ronan saw the fire leave the cardinal's eyes. "This man is broken" he thought to himself, feeling sorry for him.

They met Shakir at a viewport farther up in the cabin. The view was dark as it had been the entire ride thus far. "What am I supposed to be impressed about?" Ronan asked, being a smartass. Shakir pointed with his eyes to the window as a sudden brightness filled the cabin. The train must have emerged from the tunnel. It took his eyes a few seconds to adjust but what he saw once they, blew his mind again. "I'm starting to get sick of continually being impressed" Ronan told Shakir as he looked out over sunny fields with hills upon hills of purple hewed grass blowing in the wind. "Ok." Ronan started. "Are we still underground?" Shakir smiled. "That we are but wait! There's more." They both looked back out the viewport and watched a massive stone building begin to appear on the horizon. As the train continued to get closer, Ronan could start making out fine details of the building. Very gothic in architecture with large colored glass windows, sharp pointed spires, and covered in haunting sculptures. "Looks like a badass church" Ronan commented. "The man in charge of the whole operation lives here." Shakir began to explain. "This may be the biggest shock yet. Potentially of your life. Both of you." Shakir's voice was laced with a tiny bit of concern, not his usual. "I want you to keep an open mind through the whole thing. Don't rush to any judgements." Ronan was a tad worried at the prospect. "We've done well so far" He said. He grabbed Taylor's hand. "I think we'll be ok." Taylor interjected "How bad can it be, I mean does *the Devil* live there?" Ronan and Taylor laughed but Shakir just donned his signature smirk. "You're about to learn the truth of everything. All of your training and mental prep has been for this. Make us proud." The kids nodded. "Get all of your things and group up. We're expected."

The train slowed and finally pulled into the structure and the doors opened. Ronan and Taylor followed Shakir out and waited for the rest of the team to join them on the platform. "So, I've already spoken to the kids, but before we enter, who has never been here?" Shakir asked. A couple of hands came up from the group. "You probably know what you're in for but as I told them, keep an open mind and roll with it. You're in no danger." He laughed for a moment. "Samuel, I highly expect you to have an existential crisis, but I don't really care. Enjoy." He turned around, opened the door to the building, and everyone followed him inside.

15: THE MASK OF CATHOLICISM

The Bishop had been dreading the call he needed to make for hours now. He'd been in the office for quite a while but couldn't bring himself to do it. He had been sweating and paced the length of the office until his feet hurt. He was now sitting in the chair, staring at the tablet. He punched in the number then reluctantly hit the call button and the video conference began. He was praying the Pope wouldn't answer but it connected, and the video screen was filled with the pope's naked body and his erect penis being slobbed on by a young boy. "What can I do for you, Mike?" The pope asked. Mike doesn't answer. He just watched as the boy performed. "Bishop? I'm busy if you haven't noticed. What. Do. You. Need?" He asked again.

Mike shook it off and began "Your eminence, we were just attacked. As you predicted." He stopped to suckling noises and began speaking again to drown the noise out. "The cardinal and the book were taken. We lost them." The pope began flailing in rage and his penis thrust deep into the boy's throat causing him to gag and dry heave. The pope rolled onto his side and got up from the bed. He screamed "I told you they were coming. I gave you guards. I gave you demons. You're incompetent and everyone is going to pay." Mike watched the pope grab the young boy by his throat, strike him in the face, and throw him down onto the floor before thrusting his hard dick into the boy's ass. The young boy started to scream. The pope started screaming over his cries of pain. "Next time I see you Bishop, you will feel my wrath. More than this boy is now. Mark my words." Mike ended the video conference before anything else happened he didn't want to see. "This life is a nightmare" He thought to himself.

Once he had finished and the boy's ass was full of sacrament, the pope had him removed from his chambers. He was in no mood for games today. The shower he forced himself in felt nice but even after he had washed and robed up, his demeanor was foul. The papal employees could see his rage emanating from his body and made sure to give him a wide berth as he stalked the halls of the residence.

As he rounded a corner, Nicola noticed a group of clergymen speaking and saw the Cardinal in charge of keeping his agenda. The group quickly dispersed as he approached but the Cardinal remained, knowing it was in his best interest. "Clear the Santa Martha for me and do not make me wait long." He said to the young Cardinal. "Yes, your eminence, at once" He replied as he started moving toward the square. Nicola rushed down after him, setting him up to fail, but was slightly pleased that the chapel had already been cleared by his arrival. He would never admit it, especially with his mood today. "Leave me at once" He barked to the Cardinal. The young man bowed as he closed the doors behind him.

Nicola scurried down the center aisle and stepped up to the bell mechanism. The bell was how he summoned Poyel when he needed council in between the monthly visits. He was usually uninterested in doing so though because Poyel was generally cross when he did. He sighed, rang the bell, and hoped for the best. He crossed his arms and puffed his chest while he waited. "Why have I been summoned so soon?" A booming voice rang inside the chapel. Nicola's body language changed into that of a spineless slug. "Your excellence, Poyel, we've had a problem I seek your council on." He answered. "Well out with it. Worm." The voice commanded. Nicola tried to stand straight and tall, feeling a little bold this morning. Poyel stuck his face out into the light and looked at him which instantly reverted his stance. "Well we had… a Cardinal taken by…by *them*." The face closed his eyes and shook his head in disappointment. "You're useless." He said. "I warned you and you still couldn't figure out how to keep our integrity intact. Lucky for you, we have an inside man and are planning on squashing them for good. No thanks to ground operations, especially you." The large creature poked Nicola in the forehead and he fell over. "Continue doing whatever it is you're doing down here. We'll handle this problem through other channels" and with a quick breeze, the creature was gone.

Nicola lay there. On the floor. Defeated. Sitting in a puddle of his own piss. He had a moment of clarity though, and realized he no longer needed to deal with this issue. He could be carefree until his normal monthly meetings. "It's going to be a good day after all" he thought. Picking himself up off the floor, he dusted his robes off. He took a deep breath and let it out slowly before strolling up the aisle and out into the fresh air of the beautiful Roman afternoon they were having. He stood and enjoyed the breeze for a moment much more than the poor souls downwind of him did. A little tingle in his nether region struck a chord. It was high time for some celebration. "Fetch me some wine." He called out. "Also fetch me some boys AND girls. A party is to be had." He directed this at a young priest who happened to be nearby. "At once." The priest bowed, hoping to hide the disgust he was sure showed on his face.

16: THE IDEAL OF THE PEOPLE'S STATE

The house was an open concept and massive inside. The first thing Ronan noticed, other than the size, was the enormous Rammstein flag hanging from a high balcony down to the floor. As his gaze ventured elsewhere, he saw some suits of armor, weapons, and tons of music memorabilia tastefully placed around the lower level. The group continued to move forward and came upon a staircase. A very deep voice yelled out "Hey!" It rang through the chamber but couldn't be pinpointed until a man appeared at the top of the staircase and waved at the group. "The host of honor" Shakir told the kids. The man started to descend the stairs and as he got closer, Ronan instantly recognized him. "Is that… fucking Till?" Ronan stuttered. Shakir smiled as he greeted the man with a giant bear hug. They appeared to know each other very well and were genuinely happy to see each other.

He departed from Shakir and began walking down the line of men and women, shaking their hands. Ronan could hear him thanking them for being a part of the team. He was in shock. Of all the people in the world he would expect to see here, Till was not one of them. The kids were the last two people in line and the man approached them. "Very nice to make your acquaintance." He said. "My name is Lucifer Morningstar." Shakir came over and stood next to Lucifer. "Well, how pumped are you to meet *the devil*?" Shakir laughed as he asked. Lucifer joined in his laughter. "You know" Lucifer started saying, "that name is a nasty, nasty lie about how I really am." Ronan looked to Taylor and did so just in time to catch her as she fainted. He softly laid her body on the floor to continue the conversation. Ronan was feeling odd about this situation too. He finally said "I'm thinking that a little more explanation is needed about this whole thing" Shakir and Lucifer smiled. "And much explanation is to be had." Lucifer told him. "Shakir is going to show you and your team to the showers where you can clean up and get comfortable. We'll meet afterward, and much will be revealed." Shakir yelled "Follow me everyone. Let's. Get. Comfy!"

The cardinal looked very uncomfortable, as one could expect a member of the clergy to be, meeting Lucifer. "What about him?" Ronan asked of the cardinal. "He will be safe and allowed to clean up as well." Lucifer replied. Samuel's face brightened up. You could see that kindness wasn't a normal occurrence for this man. "I'll take him from here." Lucifer told him. "Come with me Samuel." He beckoned with his hand. "Go on Ronan, we'll catch up shortly."

Ronan knelt to wake Taylor, who came around after a few moments of his gentle prodding. "Wake up sleepy head." He told her. "What happened?" she asked. Ronan laughed. "Well we just met the devil." He helped her on her feet. "We're going to shower and get comfortable, so he can tell us a story." He let her go to make sure she was safe to stand. She nodded and began to walk with them. "Had you said that sentence to me a couple of months ago, I'd have called the state hospital." They both laughed.

The group followed Shakir through the dimly lit halls until the sound of rushing water could be heard bouncing off the walls. The hall opened into a large cavernous room. "This is beautiful" Ronan thought. "Looks like Black reach from Skyrim" He told Taylor. Translucent mushrooms the size of cars were spread around the cave giving off a comforting yellow glow to light the room. Many small pools dotted the cave as well, filled by waterfalls. This place was paradise. It was even the perfect temperature. "Where are the showers?" He asked Taylor. She giggled and pointed. He looked over and saw the team removing their gear and clothes. Ronan's cheeks got warm as a naked Shakir ran up to them. "You're not shy, are you?" He asked. Smirking as he always did. "We're family and there's no need for modesty. Come. relax with us." Ronan looked at Taylor, shrugged his shoulders, and watched as Taylor dropped her armor and exposed her beautiful, plump breasts. "Come over here once you guys get undressed." He pointed over to a large pool where the others had congregated. He ran over and jumped into the water. Ronan began to undo his armor as well and once Taylor was completely naked, she helped Ronan finish. He was hard. "This is crazy" He whispered to her. "I kind of like it" she replied, softly stroking him. "It's just a care free and loving group of people" She said with a giggle. The two walked over and joined the group at the pool.

Ronan's cock was throbbing at the situation. Every one of them was beautiful. The men were sculpted, and the woman were toned and plump in the right places. He realized he didn't even know half of their names and yet he had successfully completed a high stakes mission with them and now found himself sitting in a very clear and revealing pool of water, naked. Once he sat and scanned again, he noticed he wasn't the only one hard, so he didn't feel so odd about it anymore. Shakir swam over to them once they'd sat. "I want you two to completely wash all of your world views and ideas of what right and wrong with this water." He began. "You're to learn the truth of existence when we meet with Lucifer after this. Enjoy everything this cleansing water has to offer." He opened his palm and presented the other members of the team. Ronan noticed Maynard and a blonde girl kissing on the far side of the pool. Courtney, he thought her name is. He asked Shakir "So this is some kind of orgy?" Shakir laughed out loud. "This" He said, "This is whatever you want it to be. Clean. Relax. Decompress. No one here is judging and everyone here wants the same thing." Shakir scooted away to a man sitting near them and began to kiss him. Ronan couldn't take his eyes off what was happening but soon focused when Taylor reached down to his hard cock and stroked it. They kissed for a few moments before she stuffed it into her and he realized how wet she was. She was clearly enjoying it as much as he was. At first, he felt some sort of expected modesty being ruined but as others around them began to do the same, he focused on Taylor's little body wrapped tightly around him and not on these other emotions. "Hell" He thought, "I'm in Lucifer's house and a member of a secret organization tasked with saving the world. Why should I feel weird about this?" He brought his thoughts back to her. He loved her with all his heart and this was easily one of the most surreal and amazing experiences he'd ever been a part of. The love around him could be felt. The paradise continued to grow as a brunette began to make her way toward the couple. She gently rubbed a hand on Taylor's back to let her know she'd arrived. Taylor didn't seem fazed and kept to her work. The brunette eventually guided Taylor off his cock and placed it in her mouth. Taylor joined her, and the women shared in the work. Ronan closed his eyes and hung his head back, enjoying the experience. When the mouths stopped, he looked up to see the woman putting his dick inside her. Taylor started kissing her and rubbing her clit while she rode him. "I'm Cristina" she whispered to them while she sat there, moving her hips back and forth. "Pleasure to meet you" Ronan said, smiling. Taylor smiled too.

Ronan looked around for a moment and saw Shakir and the man he was previously kissing, having sex. It was a beautiful thing to behold. His preconceived thoughts returned for a moment, but he quickly squashed them. It was amazing because they were both locked in the moment and enjoying the experience as the rest of the team was. All judgement, all jealousy, and all preconceived notions of right and wrong had melted away. He shifted focus back to his situation and noticed Taylor was back riding him while Cristina played in the action below. Ronan felt the familiar tingle starting in his balls. As if they felt it too, Taylor hopped off and knelt with Cristina in front of him. She took her hand and gently slid it back and forth on his shaft until he finally busted all over their faces and chests.

This was a fantasy by all accounts. The situation. The location. His new life. Taylor and Cristina rinsed the cum off themselves and each took a side. Ronan snuggled them both tightly and laid there in peaceful bliss. In a daze, they laid there for a while longer while everyone else finished up. Once the other groups had successfully completed their quests, a group bath began. Friends were washing each other's backs, washing each other's hair, etc.... Ronan was surprised yet again. It may have sounded odd if he'd heard of something like this but being a part of it and seeing it happening before him, seemed completely harmless and carefree. He felt the team cohesiveness and trust had tripled in a matter of half an hour. Each member of the group now seemed so close where they had been mere strangers before. Cristina returned to where they sat with some soap. "Come here you two, let's get you cleaned up." Ronan sat amongst the two women while they helped clean each other, and then him. He couldn't help but get hard again. "Ladies" Cristina called. Two other beautiful naked women appeared. "Bath time is almost over but we've got some work to attend to, want to help?" She asked, pointing to his erection. "Sure thing" They responded in tandem. Ronan's gaze turned to Shakir for a moment who merely saluted him before getting out of the pool. "Let's do this" Taylor coached the group of goddesses'.

Once Ronan had finished again, the ladies thanked him for sharing and joined the rest of the team out of the pool. "Is this real fucking life?" He thought to himself. Taylor stood and reached a hand down to help him up. "How're you feeling babe? She asked. "Wonderful, and you?" He replied. "That... was hot." She said. "This new life. This is what I've always wanted. I've never felt like a part of something important. I feel at home here with you." Ronan gave her a kiss. "I'm happy you're here with me." Shakir yelled over, "Come on you two. Play time is over." Ronan smiled before grabbing her hand and joining the rest of them. The group was still naked and conversing when the kids arrived. The atmosphere was comfortable and jovial. They had all just slept together and were standing around naked, but it wasn't even a bit odd. He only thought of it in this way because he still felt like it should be odd, but it wasn't. "What did we just get exposed to?" Ronan asked Taylor. "No idea but I've never seen or heard of something so free and wonderful" she replied. Shakir spoke to the group "Once everyone is dried and dressed, please gather near the door so we can travel back to meet with our host." Ronan gave each of Taylor's dark nipples a kiss before getting dressed in the clothes laid out for him. An off-white shirt and pants were left, placed on top of a pair of sandals. The rest of them appeared to have been left the same. Once they all had dressed, the group followed Shakir back through the dimly lit halls to attend their meeting with Lucifer.

17: WORLDVIEW AND THE ORGANIZATION

Lucifer had been stoking a large fire in the den when the group returned from the bath. He was very happy to see them return. "Come! Come! There's plenty of room to sit" He told the group, pointing to various pieces of furniture. "Ronan. Taylor. Come sit here. Please." He pointed to a couch directly in front of him. Ronan noticed while working his way up front that everyone seemed to have a cuddle buddy, so he made sure to snuggle Taylor close when they got situated. Lucifer began once everyone had settled. "Some of you I know, some of you I don't. For those of you who don't know me, welcome to my home and thank you for supporting our cause. I'm very grateful you've decided to help. It is in everyone's best interest." Taylor kissed Ronan's cheek as Lucifer spoke. She knew this is what he'd been waiting for and she couldn't lie to herself, she was thrilled herself to find out more. "My name is Lucifer Morningstar as I told you before. I've been known by many names over the years as I am very old." He looked at Ronan. "Yes Ronan, most recently I'm known as Till Lindemann." The group laughed. Ronan joined but was intently listening.

"Human life is not from this world. It was brought here." He began. "We came here hundreds of thousands of years ago. Earth is but one of millions of farms across the galaxy." The group was honed in on his words, even Shakir, who Ronan knew must've heard this story before. "We came to turn this nutrient rich planet into our newest farm." Ronan interrupted. "What do you mean when you say farm?" Lucifer directed his gaze to Ronan and Taylor. "We colonized this world to grow and harvest human beings." He said, very matter of fact. "So where did you come from and what do you mean harvest?" Ronan fired back. Lucifer smiled. "My people, the Angeli, are from a world across the stars. Very far from here. As for human harvesting, the soul is the premier source of energy in the galaxy. Would you require any further explanation at this time?" Lucifer asked, smiling. "Not yet, I'm tracking" Ronan replied, smiling himself.

"So, we came here to build a new farm." He started back up "Our ship made the journey safely and we successfully created the first group of humans in our lab. The humans the Angeli create are much like your cattle population; Alive and coherent but no thoughts of any merit." A couple of sighs rang out from around the circle. "This was my first mission away from home and we weren't fully aware of what it meant to start a farm before getting here. It's a messy and disturbing job creating humans in this way. Once the bodies were created, the older of us would use them and their orifices for pleasure. They couldn't say anything and just took it. It was wrong. It felt wrong and I wasn't the only one who thought so. A group of us banded together and snuck into manufacturing the night before we were supposed to release the humans onto the ground. We gave the group of humans sentient thought and made them free thinking. We destroyed the machine afterward."

A collective gasp sounded off. "You've all heard the story of Adam and Eve?" The group nodded individually. "Well, they were two of the humans in the first production. When we gave them their thoughts, Eve was enamored with Adam, but he went and fucked the production manager's wife in her sleep that night. Angeli pussy is your forbidden fruit in the story and the shame afterward was Eve's jealousy of the whole matter." Everyone laughed. Maynard asked after "So all of the bible stories are true?" Lucifer nodded and answered. "A good majority are based in fact. So anyway" He continued "We were all put on trial for our sabotage and exiled from the ship." Another of the team, Kurt, Ronan believed his name was, spoke up. "How you are fallen from heaven, O Lucifer, son of the morning!" Shakir laughed. "Someone payed good attention in scripture class." The group laughed. "Nice job" He told him. Lucifer remarked "Oh yes. My famous fall." He laughed. "They actually just dropped us off and deserted us on the ground. I was happy to be free of them and their cruelty, but it wasn't easy to get here. We've been fighting them ever since. Welcome to the fight!" He exclaimed. They group cheered.

Lucifer told the group "Please feel free to go get some rest. We'll be leaving for Hyperborea in the morning so rest up. The prisoner is safe in his cell, so no one need worry. Go be free. Ronan and Taylor, please stay so we can talk further."

The kids remained comfortable on the couch as the group thanked the man for his hospitality and retreated for the night. Shakir stayed with them as well. Ronan whispered to Taylor "I can only imagine what's coming. Also wondering if the surprises will ever end." She giggled. "Buckle up son" Lucifer told Ronan. "Shit's about to get wild" Shakir added.

18: THE FIRST PERIOD OF HIS STRUGGLE

Lucifer sat on the couch next to the kids and Shakir followed suit. "What do you know of your family?" Lucifer asked Ronan. "Well, mom and dad are back in Hyperborea." He told him. "Not your adopted parents but your blood family" Lucifer clarified. Ronan thought hard for a moment. "I only know what Charles briefly told me when I first arrived in Hyperborea. I don't know anything more than that." Lucifer solemnly shook his head in acknowledgment. "What if I told you I knew one of your family members?" Taylor perked up. Ronan seemed indifferent. "Well, I'd listen to what you had to say." Ronan replied. Shakir piped in "You don't sound very interested." Ronan shook his head "I'm still finding it hard to come to terms with the fact they didn't abandon me. The Corver's are amazing and I'm happy they're mine. No one else cared. At least it's what I thought all this time" Taylor rubbed her hand across his back. "I didn't know you felt that way, I'm so sorry" She said.

"I'm sure they kept it from you to save you from the uncertainty, but you weren't abandoned Ronan. Not even close." Lucifer placed his hand on Ronan's shoulder. "The day you were born was the happiest day of your parents' life." Ronan began to perk up. "Lukas had always wanted kids. As soon as he met Asuka, I knew it was bound to happen quickly. They were head over heels in love." Ronan was blank for a moment. He'd only heard these names once. It took him a moment to come back to reality to ask, "I've only heard those names once before this and they still sound so foreign." Shakir and Lucifer both nod. "They were members of our society. Like the Corver's and Reis'." Shakir added. "I fought beside them many times." Lucifer reflected "We all did. They were both great warriors and people."

Ronan sat up on the edge of the sofa and Taylor sat up with him. "Tell me more" he demanded. "What happened to them? Where are they? You're the devil. You must know something." Lucifer answered, "Well I feel like you've got a solid idea of how this operation works." Ronan nodded in acknowledgment. "So it was early 2001 and we were in the desert, where it all began, trying to stop this war from happening. As you also know very well, we failed. We lost your parents and a few other warriors in that fight." Ronan was deep in thought. "You didn't find their bodies, so where did they go?" Ronan asked. "Well that place is riddled with stargates, so your guess is as good as mine. We occasionally go back to look and keep all the lines of communication open that we safely can. We hope to see them again someday too." Ronan sighed. "You were only an infant and Emma was unable to have children of her own. It seemed fitting." Lucifer continued. Ronan was still thoughtful and silent for a moment longer. He was having trouble organizing his thoughts. "So if they're gone, who do you know from my family?" He finally asked. Shakir laughed. "Oh you didn't know that Lucie here is your Great Grand-Dad?" Lucifer punched Shakir in the arm but he was smiling. "Always taking the glory for yourself." He turned attention to Ronan. "Lukas was my grandson. Which makes you the same."

Ronan quickly stood. "So the devil and all of that is real. That I can stomach in an odd way." Lucifer and Shakir were listening. "My parents didn't abandon me. That brings me an internal calm I didn't know I needed. The fact that I'm spawn to Satan though..." He began to get dizzy, but Taylor helped him find his seat before he fell. "That is an odd truth to try and accept. Wow" He laid down, his head on Taylor's lap. "To someone who had no idea of the real world prior to a few months ago, I can understand that." Lucifer said. "Though as you've seen, and we've been trying to show you, we're not what people think. We're fighting for the survival of humanity even amidst all the poison that is being spread. I may be thousands of years old, but I'm just a normal person." He smiled. "I mean it's not really that weird considering" Taylor directed at Ronan. "No, no I guess it's not." He replied. "I just don't know what this means. For my life."

Shakir looked at him. "It changes nothing. It only means you have more people in your life to care for you and more good people to interact with. You're related to humanities last hope. None of this would be possible without him." Lucifer picked up "Oh hush. I organize it because I was a part of it. You guys do all the work. He's right though." Directed at Ronan. "I'm not going to make an awkward situation. Now you know and can do whatever you want with that knowledge. The fight rages on and as long as you're on our side, we can deal with this at any time." Ronan felt comfortable with that answer. "I'm ready for bed." Ronan said looking at Taylor. "Shakir, would you show them to their room?" Lucifer asked. "As his *majesty* commands." Shakir responded famously. "Sometimes, I wish I hadn't saved your soul." Lucifer responded with an exaggerated wink. Shakir and Lucifer hugged before departing to the sleeping area. "Sleep well children" Lucifer called to them as they left. "You too!" Taylor replied. Once they had left the room, Shakir asked "How's this sitting with you?" Ronan took a moment to answer. "You know, Till Lindemann is my grandfather. Plus he's Satan. That's actually metal as fuck." They all laughed as Shakir stopped in front of a door. "This is your room here" he told them. "Nighty night love birds."

Samuel couldn't believe the accommodations he had here. Nicer than he ever had at the church and as a prisoner to boot. He knew the attitude from his captors was warranted. He knew what the church stood for, but he was as much a victim as anyone. Abuse was nothing new to him anyway. They may have hated him but at least they weren't hurting him. He'd most definitely have been hurt if he was at the Vatican. This was a nice reprieve.

He explored and decided these chambers were nicer than the Popes own in Rome. Once he had explored all corners of his room, he decided to take a much-needed shower. There was actual lavender growing in the bathroom which mixed with the steam from the shower. He felt drowsy and sat himself down, propped in the shower and fell asleep. He woke to someone standing over him. He was startled when the person grabbed his arm and helped him to his feet. Samuel started to panic once he came to and ran out of the bathroom butt naked. He remembered once he reached the door that it was locked, he'd already tried it, and so he hid behind a large piece of furniture. A voice began speaking to him in his mind. "Cardinal, please relax. You are a prisoner while here but you are safe from physical and mental harm. Of that I can assure you." Samuel stopped panicking. He stood and saw the man who had helped him to his feet in the shower. It was the man they had called Lucifer earlier.

"You're comfortable?" The man asked him. Samuel nodded. "I'd like to offer you a truce. You're only a prisoner for your safety. You've proven to be very relaxed compared to some of your colleagues. You shouldn't fear us. We do things much differently than you're used to and you'll be treated with dignity and respect as long as you return it. Is that fair?" Samuel nodded and replied. "Very. Thank you." Lucifer pointed to a silver tray near the bed. "A warm meal awaits." He laughed. "Some clothes too." Samuel had forgotten he was naked. He started to cover himself but gave up the effort and just let it be. "We leave for our capital in the morning." Lucifer told him. "Sleep well. You're very safe here." The man bowed before exiting the room.

Samuel didn't even bother putting clothes on. He hopped up onto the bed and had his dinner. He devoured it in minutes. Must've been too stressed to realize how hungry he was. Slipping under the covers, he quickly passed out and slept like he had never slept before in his life; warm, comfortable, and safe.

19: THE STRONG IS WEAKEST WHEN ALONE

Not a single member of the team woke that morning thinking of anything else. They'd all had the best night's sleep they'd ever had. They began to trickle downstairs one by one seeking some breakfast or at least an idea as to their direction. Most of them had been soldiers for a very long time and felt odd not being given direction for their day. The freedom seemed suspicious. They all eventually made their way to the den which was decorated like an illustrated fairy tale. A long wooden table which spanned the entire room was lined with piles of breakfast food. The group was overjoyed and dug right in without waiting for direction.

Ronan woke peacefully too. Rolling over, he gently placed his hand on Taylor's thigh. She was still sleeping because he could hear her gently snoring. He laid there thinking of how his life had changed. Only a few months ago he had no idea of the real world. He was part of the normal, boring world and he had no girlfriend. He woke up today a key part of a secret multi-national, no, a multi-planetary force of justice fighters. He now had an amazing girlfriend and had found that he wasn't abandoned as he thought. He was adopted into this world and his only living blood relative was the devil. What a change a few months can make. He chuckled, and Taylor stirred. He watched as she rolled over, all the while admiring her body as it moved. He ran his hand up her side and over one of her breasts before smacking her butt lightly. "Good morning beautiful" He told her. She smiled warmly, her eyes still closed. "Good morning, how long have you been awake?" She asked. "Not that long" He replied. "I've been laying here thinking about how crazy life has gotten. How lucky I am to have you." He kissed her stomach.

"But don't you know that I'm the lucky one? You treat me like a queen." She ran her fingers through his hair. "You are my queen. Apparently, we're to rule hell." They both laughed. "Lucifer being my Grandfather and all." He added. "You've always been my rock Ronan. The only light in my life. I'm happy you brought me along on this journey with you." They start to kiss. "You think we have time for some…" He raised his eyebrows a couple times. "We're the king and queen of hell, we have time" she answered him before flipping herself into his lap.

The kids ran into Shakir in the hallway on their way downstairs. "Slept well I presume?" He asked them. "Best sleep I think I've ever gotten" Taylor responded. Ronan nodded in agreement. "Lucie was always good for that. He knows some otherworldly knacks." Shakir smiled. "How long have you known him?" Ronan asked. "A very, very long time" Was all they got out of him before they got to the den. He stopped in the doorway to let the kids pass and for the first time, Ronan noticed the scars Shakir had on his forehead. Little indents right on his hairline. His mind was running wild with an idea so crazy that he just shut it down. He followed Shakir and Taylor through the door.

The team had already dug in to the amazing feast laid out on a long table. They stopped eating when they noticed Shakir entered the room. "Continue, please" He told them. "We've got an amazing group of people in the Thule." He said to the kids as they began to scope the table out. "Many have lost everything but continue to fight because it's the right thing to do." He reflected as he piled bacon on his plate. "What would the world be like if it were up to the Thule? How would it be different?" Ronan asked him. Shakir turned and looked at him.

He then replied very loudly "Thule! What do you want for the world?" The team stood from their seats and began to speak one by one. "No homeless people." One of the women said from the back. "A unified world state with a fair ruling body" Maynard added. Taylor stepped forward "No more hate!" The group cheered at her addition. She smiled shyly. Ronan spoke up. "NO more war." Lucifer appeared through the door and joined in Ronan's standing ovation. Shakir added "Love, free of chains and judgement." The room exploded. Shakir looked over to Ronan and whispered to him "This is what we stand for. This is what we will bring to the world. Love and peace. Fair treatment. Equality." Ronan never felt more at home. It's all he'd ever hoped for in the world. Taylor looked happy too. The static in the room was electrifying. These were his people and he would do whatever necessary to help them finish this war.

Lucifer addressed the room after they'd finished with the breakfast feast. "Don't worry about cleanup." A couple of the group laughed. There was a decent sized mess. "We're headed back to the city today with our prisoner. Gear up and be ready shortly. There's no rush but there is an event tonight we absolutely have to be back for." He smiled at Ronan. "You'll want to be back for it. I promise." He whispered to Ronan. "What is it?!" Ronan asked excitedly. "I've invited some of my friends to come down and play." He said with a smile. "Holy shit, is Rammstein playing for us tonight?" Lucifer just kept smiling and let Ronan's imagination run wild. Lucifer excused himself from the den. "I'll meet you outside with the prisoner shortly." Ronan was having a mild panic attack when Taylor and Shakir came over to him. "What's wrong babe?" She asked. "I'm pretty sure Rammstein is playing in the city tonight." He regurgitated quickly. Shakir laughed. "They're not alone." He

started, gauging Ronan's interest. The two of them notice
Ronan enter another dimension and giggled as they tried to
imagine what he was thinking.

Finding out Till is the devil AND his grandfather was
badass. Finding out the truth of existence was badass too.
Finding out that he will be hanging out with Rammstein tonight
though, was by far the coolest thing to happen since joining the
Thule.

20: THE CONFLICT WITH HOLY FORCES

It took some time, but Taylor finally got Ronan back to the room and back to reality. The team dispersed to gear up and get ready for the journey back to the city. They were escorting the Cardinal back for the formal interrogation. Shakir told them he didn't predict any issues, but they were going with guns blazing just in case. The kids got into a shower to rinse off the sleep and Ronan was done first. His pants were half on as she came out of the bathroom naked. Ronan loved watching Taylor get dressed. She was a goddess among women. He just sat on the bed and watched her booty bounce as she walked over to her armor. She had to dance into her pants which was an activity he was fond of, especially while she was topless. He stood before she had time to put a shirt on and grabbed her by the small of her back. He pulled her in for a kiss and a caressed one of her boobs. "I love you inside and out and I hope showing you every chance I get isn't annoying." He told her. She blushed. "Not at all." He smiled and let her go so she could finish getting ready. He had to do the same.

Samuel woke and felt like a million bucks as he laid there, enjoying his solace. He slept through the night for the first time he could ever remember. No night visits, no demons, and all in the house of the devil. He was having a slight internal conflict at the whole thing but felt much too good to care about the small details. He was being respected and enjoying every second of it. As he sat up, he noticed another tray at the foot of his bed. There was a warm plate of breakfast food waiting for him. This was a miracle. He'd never had it so good in his life.

He got himself out of bed after eating and found clothes had been left out for him. He dressed in the clothes he found and looked at himself in the mirror as he passed. It was hard not to notice how much better actual clothes felt and looked on him. He'd been wearing his religious garb his entire life. The door to his room opened while he was admiring himself and Lucifer entered. "Good morning Samuel. I trust you slept well?" He asked. "I did. The best I ever have as I can recall." Lucifer looked happy. "It pleases me to hear that Sam. Can I call you Sam?" He asked. "No one ever has. I kind of like it. Please do." He replied "Well Sam" Lucifer started, "We'd like your help in saving the world. You know firsthand what the church is really about." Samuel became a little defensive. "What do you want from me?" Lucifer moved closer and put his hand on Sam's shoulder. "I'd like you to be a guest of ours and come to our capital. Let us show you what we're like and what we're planning. You've got very important information that could help us." Sam shook his head "But I don't know anything or even who you really are." Lucifer smiled. "Well I am exactly who I say I am. I am Lucifer Morningstar. Your thoughts on me and historical events has been warped by the church but that's not your fault. As for what you can do, your daily routine in Rome is all we need. Worry not about it now. We'll talk once you see what we're planning and only if you decide to join our team." Sam looked concerned. "You. You want me to join your team? But why?" He asked. "Well, you'll be very helpful to us with your inside knowledge and we love and accept all good people. You're a good person in there aren't you?" Sam was silent before skulking over to bed and sat on it. "I'm not sure if I know what it is to be a good person. I don't hurt people if that's what it means." Lucifer came over to him and looked him dead in the face. "That is certainly a big part. Helping people in need is also a big part. How would you like to help all the little boys in the same spot you were when you were young? All the men in your position until yesterday? Get back at the Pope? The church?" Sam stood. "I'll come with you but I'm not sure about anything yet" He said, guarded. "Good! We're getting ready to go. Come with me if you're ready?" Lucifer asked. Sam nodded. "I'm ready."

Geared up and armed, the kids met the rest of the team down in the lobby area where they first entered the house. The group dynamic had vastly changed since the last time they were gathered for a mission. The air was much more relaxed. The energy in the room was very cohesive and familiar. Ronan thought it felt good and he asked Taylor if she noticed it. She nodded in agreement. "Yes. This feels good. Such an odd thing to be feeling but we're almost a single mind. That's what I feel anyway" she said. Shakir appeared behind them, seemingly out of nowhere "The Thule is pretty famous for our *team building exercises*." He draped his arms around the kid's necks. "We're ready to move. Are you?" They both nodded. "Where's the cardinal?" Taylor asked. As if on cue, Lucifer and the Cardinal appeared at the top of the staircase where Lucifer had first appeared. The team tightened up, ready for anything but Lucifer put his hand up. "This is Sam, everybody. He was born a victim and did what he needed to survive. He is a guest of the Thule and we are his escort back to Hyperborea. He will cause no issues."

Ronan could sense the distrust, but the team did as instructed and relaxed. Shakir moved toward the center of the room. "Form up. We're moving out. Sam is an important tool in our fight. He is to be protected at all costs." The team grunted as a unit and created a circle with Sam in the center. "We don't anticipate any issues as the enemy has no idea where we are, but the earth is *dark and full of terrors*." Shakir giggled as he spoke. Ronan laughed and whispered to Taylor. "He reminds me of myself. Smartass. All. The. Time." She kissed him on the cheek. "You're right. Neither of you take anything seriously." He kissed her back. "I take you seriously. Us." He said. She smiled. "I never doubted it."

The team moved as a group through the doors they'd entered when they first arrived and found themselves back on the train platform. The demon train was waiting for them and had been turned around, now facing another direction. Seeing the train in this light, Ronan thought it looked less scary but was still a very menacing sight. "That train is awfully Steampunk" He whispered to Taylor. "I love it" He said. The train was technologically advanced but now that he could see it, the look was very old with lots of copper and mechanical fixtures. He continued to admire the train until the group had fully loaded onto the train. The Cardinal was sitting with them as a guest now and not a prisoner. He looked nice enough Ronan thought, but only time would tell. Once they had all settled, the train let out a whistle which was actually terrifying and began to lurch forward.

The mission had been a success and he'd been opened up to many new experiences since he left the city. He was happy to get back to Hyperborea, so he could tell his parents about everything. He wondered who knew about Lucifer. He pulled Taylor a little closer, so she was comfortable. As he sat there, he began to doze off. His last thought before falling into deep sleep was what else would he find out on this journey?

21: PROPAGANDA AND ORGANIZATION

The train ride was over before Ronan realized because he had fallen into a deep sleep. Taylor roused him as it started to slow. They pulled into the same station that Shakir and he had a few months before. It was all very different this time though. It now felt familiar and like home. They followed the team out onto the platform, still surrounding Samuel, shielding him, even though they were safe in the city. Shakir stalked out of the train, followed by Lucifer. "Get Sam safely to command where we can begin to plan this attack." Lucifer commanded. "Ronan and Taylor, get back home and let everyone know you're ok." He added. The team took off with same swiftly while the kids stayed put. Shakir told them "Meet us back at command in the morning. We'll have a plan together by then which we'll present to the community. Have a good night!" Shakir began to head in the same direction as the team, off toward the command building. Lucifer walked up beside the kids. "The Corvers have already been told that you know. I hope someday soon we can see more of each other. I'm happy to finally have you in this fight. Our family was destined to end it." Lucifer also left them on the platform and was headed toward command. Ronan stood there, lost in thought. So much had taken place over the last couple of days. Taylor woke him from his daze. "I need a shower. Let's get home. You could help me." She kissed his cheek. "Yea!" He replied. "Do you know how to get home from here?" She laughed as she asked him. "Pretty sure I do" He replied, slightly skeptical. "This way" He stated and started moving.

Emma was in the kitchen washing a large pot she needed for dinner. She was thinking "I wish I knew when Henrik was coming home. The kids are coming back tonight and I'm making a huge dinner, some help would be nice." The Reis' were in the living room relaxing but she didn't want to bother them. Karma had told her to let her know when it was time to start peeling potatoes though. She finished rinsing the pan and stopped for a moment to think. A lot had changed in the last few months. They had led as normal a life as possible with Ronan. It was what they decided would be best after they lost his parents. Fate had already decided though and it seemed he was meant to be a part of this after all. She put the pot on the stove and found her way to the living room to let Karma know she was ready for some help. As she rounded the corner though, she slowed when she saw that they were sleeping in each other's arms on the couch. She just watched them for a few moments and thought: After all they'd been through, how lovely it was they still enjoyed each other enough to fall asleep holding one another amidst all this chaos. She left them in peace and returned to the kitchen to start prepping dinner.

The kids began travelling toward the spire of the command building because all the other roads branched out from there. Ronan was spacing out for most of the walk. Taylor was having fun prodding him. "Are you super excited for the concert tonight?" She asked. He shook it off and picked up the pace. "Excited?! Excited?" His eyes got wide. "I'm related to Till, who is the devil, and Rammstein is coming here to hang out and play. Yes. I'm excited." He smiled at her. "I'm sorry. I'm trying to focus but there's just so much to think about." She rubbed his back as they walked. "I know there is but don't forget I'm here for you, like you've always been here for me." He nodded. "I know, and I appreciate you. I'm feeling ok with all of it, I'm just trying to organize it all." "Well, just let me know if there is anything I can do for you" She added. He stopped walking and hugged her. "I will".

Emma had a pot of potatoes boiling on the stove and she was cutting up some chicken when she heard the front door open. She dropped the knife and quickly rinsed her hands before jogging into the entry way. The kids were hanging up their coats when she entered. "Ronan! Taylor!" She said excitedly as she ran over to hug them both. "Hi mom" Ronan said unenthusiastically. Taylor smiled big. "Emma!" She returned, matching Emma's energy. "I'm so happy you're ok! How did it go?" Emma asked them. "I know what you learned on this trip." She said before they could answer. "We can talk about that later or not at all. Up to you but I'm curious about the rest!" She ushered them into the kitchen, so they could talk while cooking dinner. "Well, the mission was a success." Ronan started to explain. "Everyone on our team came back alive and we got the guy we went for" Ronan sat on a stool. Taylor pulled one up next to him. "We ended up going underground and taking some demon train" Taylor added. Emma was smiling. "Where'd the train bring you?" Emma entertained. Ronan smiled. "You're loving this." He said to her. She pointed to herself "Who me?" She laughed. "You're right, I am. I was born into this so it was never anything exciting to me. It was normal life. It's interesting to hear it from someone who never knew any of it was real." Ronan answered her initial question. "Well we ended up at Satan's castle who turns out to be my Great Grandfather. That was an interesting night." He stopped and smiled. Taylor nudged him and giggled. "You can skip that part." Emma told them. "I know full well what happens down there." Emma finished while laughing. The kids looked horrified. Taylor changed the direction of the conversation "So we found all that out and came back here for some big meeting." Ronan patted her on the back in appreciation. "Yea that's where dad is. Meeting with the big wigs trying to figure out what our next move is." Emma explained as she was mashing potatoes. "Why don't you guys go get cleaned up? Be quiet though, the Reis' are napping!" The kids stood up and made their way into the hallway as Emma continued with dinner. They snuck by the living room on route to the stairs and saw the old couple sleeping. Taylor whispered "aww" to Ronan as they pass by. He let her pass him and go first up the stairs. "Let's get you upstairs and clean Ms. Quinn" He whispered to her. She blushed and made her way upstairs, dropping clothes as she went.

22: FUNDAMENTAL IDEAS OF ENTERTAINMENT

After an amazing shower, as most were with Taylor, the kids went back to the room to find some suitable clothing for the seriously insane concert they were going to attend tonight. All of Ronan's tees were still in Boston so he wasn't sure what he was going to wear. He found a clean pair of jeans and his converse, so he threw those on and went to the closet to find a shirt. After digging through some stuff hanging up, he found a box on the floor. He opened it and gasped. There was a sleeveless black vest with a Rammstein patch on the left breast. It was a perfect fit for his night. He grabbed it out of the box and stood up to go show Taylor. He turned just as she was walking out of the bathroom. He stopped what he was doing and just admired the bounce of her curves for a moment. She went out of sight for a second and he came back to reality. She reappeared with pants on but no top and he fell back into his daze again at the sight of her boobs. Her olive skin glowed and he couldn't help but enjoy it every time he saw it. She called to him a couple times before he came back to reality. "Mr. Corvers? Like you've never seen my tits before" she laughed. He shook his head and proceeded to show her the vest. "Check this thing out!" He said excitedly. "Wow babe!" She replied. "Where'd that come from?" Answering her question, Lucifer walked into the room "I brought some of my old things over for you. Figured your clothes were still in Boston." He walked closer to Ronan. "Put it on!" Lucifer exclaimed. Ronan unzipped it to put the vest on and realized Taylor still had no shirt on. He laughed to himself, obviously no one cared. He threw his arms into it and zipped it back up. He walked over to a mirror to check it out. Lucifer walked up behind him. "That is the vest Paul wore on a recent tour. Fits you good. He'll be pleased you're going to use it." Ronan's face got all warm. It was starting to hit him. Till was his grandfather and he was going to get to see Rammstein live tonight. "Where are the guys?" Ronan asked, unable to hide his excitement. "Should be here anytime." He answered. "It's not a long trip from Berlin. Finish getting ready, both of you, and come meet me downstairs. We'll walk over together." He bowed and left the room. "How excited are you for your life right now?" She asked while putting her bra on." He had nearly uncontrollable excitement brimming, ready to spill over. "I'm trying to keep it in check" He smiled. "I don't want to fanboy too hard."

The kids quickly finished getting ready and jolted downstairs to meet Lucifer. As they rounded the corner, they saw another man in the kitchen with Emma and Lucifer. His hair was long and messy, and he was wearing a kilt. "Are you fucking kidding me?" was all Ronan could muster. Lucifer laughed, noticing they'd joined them. "Yes Ronan, I got my friend Jonathan Davis to come with his band too." Jonathan turned around and smiled at the kids. "Killer line up, huh?" He asked Ronan. It took him a moment to craft a response. "Yea, you could say I'm pretty excited for it." He said. The room laughed. Lucifer told him "It's ok. We all know how you really feel." Ronan balled his hands into fists and screamed "So let's get over there!" Jon picked up and finished his drink in one gulp and threw the can out. He burped and exclaimed "Hell yea, I'm ready." Lucifer also chimed in "I am too. Let's get a move on." Emma said to the kids "I'll see you over there. The Reis' are coming too." Taylor laughed. "They're coming?" She asked. "Everyone in the Thule loves live music and when we party, everyone comes to the celebration." Emma filled her in. "Fair enough" Taylor smiled as she responded. "Catch you over there ma" Ronan called out as the group headed toward the door. He was now walking toward a festival show, in Hell, with Till Lindemann and Jonathan Davis. "Who else are we gonna meet?" He asked himself.

Apparently, the capital pyramid building housed a giant audience chamber that doubled as a live venue when needed. The Thule used it mainly for meetings and demonstrations but by Jonathan's account, a hell of a stage. Taylor noticed the streets were completely bare as the boys talked music and asked, "Where is everyone?" Lucifer pointed toward the building and said "They're all at the capital anxiously awaiting the show. Emma wasn't lying when she said everyone here gets excited about our live shows." He laughed. Ronan's excitement was getting hard to hide. "So where are we sitting? Ronan asked, fueling his already growing energy. Jon replied to him "Sitting? You guys are family so you're watching from side stage. Really no other place you belong." Taylor watched his face light up. "We have a really good time hanging before the show then we watch each other from side stage. Best seats in the house." Lucifer looked at his watch. "The guys should be here by now, getting ready. You're all welcome to come have a shot or two with us." Ronan doesn't say anything, but his expression tells it all. "I'll take whatever you give me but I'm just happy to be hanging out." Ronan finally spit out. "Maybe you'll be called out during someone's set to play" Lucifer suggested, as if he had some inside info. Ronan nearly had a stroke at the thought. "I may have told some of friends you know a lot of the material tonight so someone may call you out during a song." Lucifer added. "But how do you know that?" Ronan asked, in a daze. "I'm *Satan*" he replied with a laugh. "I know." Everyone laughed.

The capital building was fast approaching on the horizon and Ronan could hear music playing. Ready to stroke out for the umpteenth time today, he realizes it's not live and breathes a silent sigh of relief. He didn't want to miss a thing. They reached the side doors and entered the familiar hustle of the command room. Over to the left was the staircase that brought them down to Victor's area and all around them was the brain of the operation. They'd never ventured past this room but followed Lucifer and Jon into a new area beyond. It was a large hallway they entered, and it began to grow outward the farther they walked. People were moving cases of equipment and gear around. The music was loud back here, he loved it. Ronan was scanning for anyone he knew but had yet to see anyone else of note. He continued to follow the group through the controlled chaos of the backstage area and he walked into Taylor when they stopped. "Hey pay attention!" She laughed. "My B." He said, laughing. "Are you ready to meet the guys?" Lucifer asked Ronan. His eyes got big, but he couldn't say anything in response. Lucifer just smiled and opened the door. "I'll catch you guys soon" Jonathan told them before continuing to walk down the hall.

Ronan waved as he entered the room, fully expecting to finally have the stroke that was pending and die. As they rounded the corner, he saw them. Oliver was benching some weights, Schneider was in the mirror doing something with his eye makeup, Flake was sitting on the couch with his right leg crossed over his left reading a book, and Richard was sitting opposite Paul on another set of chairs, laughing about something. His heart fluttered. Richard stood when noticed them and called out "Till! You made it." Paul stood next and gave his best Rick Flair "WOOOOOOOO!" Everyone laughed. Olli put the bar up and sat up to greet them. "Machen Sie sich bereit! (Get ready!)" He directed at Lucifer. "Oh shit" Lucifer replied, "Where's my stuff?" Flake pointed over to a container stacked near the mirror. Lucifer grabbed Ronan by the shoulders and pulled him in front of him. "This is my grandson Ronan. He's a premier fan so be nice to him." The band laughed. Lucifer grabbed his stuff and disappeared behind another door. Ronan goes right up to Paul and Richard. "The new Emigrate album is amazing." He blurted out to RZK. His excitement could be seen on his face. Paul suggested "Atme tief ein (Take a deep breath)" while laughing. Ronan took a deep breath and felt a little better. Richard guided him to the couch. "Are you excited to see the show tonight?" He asked Ronan. "I'm thrilled at this whole thing" he said. "Are you guys playing Weisses Fleisch?" Schneider picked up a set list on the vanity and looked over it for a moment. "Nein" He answered while shaking his head. Richard asked Flake "Would it mess up your sequences to add it?" Flake shook his head. "Well we can play that. If you'd like?" Breaking all possibility, Ronan lit up even more. "It's such a jam when you guys play it live." Flake looked mildly displeased as he usually did. "Ich liebe tanzen (I love dancing)" He said while shrugging his shoulders. They all laughed. Lucifer reappeared with his stage gear on. "The first band is about to start" He told everyone. Ronan looked around and noticed that they were all in their performance clothes. "Who's up first?" Ronan asked the group. "Some friends from Ohio followed by some extreme metal from Britain." Lucifer sounded excited. Ronan had a few ideas but would hold off the speculation. He just wanted to go check it out. Standing up with energy, the others followed suit.

They shuffled for the door and entered the hall just as the lights cut and orchestrated music began to play loudly. He recognized it as a group of people walked by. The overheads had been cut but a few in the group had flashlights to light the path. Ronan got a flash of who it was. He noticed Diablo's horns and Skinny's dreads. "Mushroomhead" He said. His existence at this very moment seemed fulfilled. He and the band followed them to the stage and hung back to watch. The curtain was up but you could hear the crowd going wild when the stadium lights cut out. The curtain dropped as the circus like keyboards of QWERTY started playing from Stitches' sampler. Ronan finally got a good look at everyone both onstage and in the crowd. Mushroomhead was in their black light outfits and looked visually stunning as always. He turned to investigate the audience and couldn't even see how many people were in the auditorium. It was packed. He believed his mom that every single citizen of Hyperborea was in here. The energy was electrifying.

Ronan thoroughly enjoyed Mushroomhead's set from side stage. He'd seen them plenty of times before but never like this. They congratulated them on a great set as they exited the stage and the roadies began clearing gear as the curtain was pulled back up. "You said the next act was from Britain, right?" Ronan asked Lucifer. He nodded. "I'm fairly certain you'll be interested to see them this close." Ronan's mind was running wild with ideas. They move out of the way as techs started to bring equipment and staging by them. He saw a gorgeous woman setting up a keyboard next to the drum kit. He thought he recognized her but couldn't place her. As he watched more stage go up, he started to see some very gothic characters grouping on the other side of the stage. He decided to just keep watching but he was pretty sure he knew what was happening. The group across the way began to put on instruments and stretch as the woman triggered an orchestrated intro track and it hit him. Dani stalked out with the rest of the band: Cradle of Filth. His day continued to get better as he watched these British monsters play through some amazing tunes. They end their set with "From Cradle to Enslave" and left the stage to thunderous applause as the curtain rose again. Lucifer asked Ronan "Well what do you think so far? You happy with it?" Ronan stuttered "This is probably the most amazing thing to ever happen to me." Lucifer laughed "Well I'm glad you think so. I can't wait for to see what else is coming."

Taylor had already noticed Johannes and his ringleader get up but figured she'd let Ronan see what was next on his own. She wanted to see his surprise and happiness. The techs had cleared the stage and set up a new drum kit with some yellow and red designs. A couple of people enter the stage from the opposite side as Jonas walked by Ronan and started playing the "For the Swarm" intro riff. The band kicked in and Johannes walked up behind Ronan. He handed Ronan a mic and gestured him to follow. He was a natural entertainer Taylor noticed. Walked right out and threw his hands up to get the crowd going before singing the first line "K-O-wardwardwardwardward coward". Ronan was exhilarated to be on stage with one of his favorite bands. After the song was done with, Johannes introduced him to the Thule and the crowd went wild! Ronan walked back to stand with Rammstein and watch the rest of the set while Tim started playing the opening riff for "Hail the Apocalypse". Avatar killed the set as usual and left the stage as the curtain was pulled back up once again.

Ronan noticed a hulk of a man with long black hair and a full beard watching from the opposite side of the stage. He was standing next to a smaller man with a golden grill. At the rate the night was going, Ronan knew who they were and couldn't believe his luck. More techs bust out of nowhere and began moving the stage around for the next band. The techs build a set that has a dual spiral staircase in the middle of the stage and it confirmed his suspicions. He'd seen this stage before. Slipknot was about to play. He was just looking at Mick and Sid. This night was incredible and getting better by the minute. Unlike newer shows he'd, Sid started spinning the intro from the self-titled album. The rest of the band took their position on the stage. Corey walked over to Ronan and gave him a fist bump as Jay did the 4 count into "(Sic)". Slipknot played with a fiery intensity through many of their best songs. The curtain pulled back up as they exited the stage. Jonathan caught Corey on the way off the stage and spoke to him for a minute. "Oh shit" Taylor said. "Jonathan's back." He joined the group after Corey had left. "Corey's down to perform our new song tonight!" He said excitedly. Ronan caught some of his excitement "So you guys are playing next?" He asked. "Hell yes! What should we open with?" Jonathan asked the group. Paul looked at Ronan and asked, "Du gut? (You good?)" "Me?" Ronan asked back. "Ja!" Paul said with a laugh. "Twist!" Ronan called out without a second thought. "Noted" Jonathan said with a nod. He headed over to the center of the stage to fill the rest of the band in. Ronan could see Fieldy and Head talking to Jonathan. He couldn't believe this shit. As if being told you're related to Satan and the fact that he was the singer of Rammstein wasn't enough of a revelation, he was surrounded by every one of his favorite bands. Joining the Thule had changed his life forever.

Ronan noticed Ray pop onto the drum kit and everyone else was up front. Jonathan looked over their way and winked at him. As Jonathan began "You're not the right one dumb damn rapper", the curtain fell, and the band started playing "Twist" per Ronan's request. Ronan's group jammed for the entire set. "Korn is amazing live" Lucifer said aloud. All heads bob in agreement. Someone walked up behind them toward the end of "Got the Life". Ronan looked back to see Corey Taylor standing with the group, rocking out himself. The song ended, and Corey moved up next to Ronan. "You've heard their new album, right?" He asked him. "Hell yea I have" Ronan answered. "This is the first time we've ever done this together live. Let me know what you think after." Corey patted Ronan on the shoulder as he ran out to perform "A Different World" with Korn. Live collaboration was one of Ronan's favorite things. This song sounded so good. It was one of his top three from the album. Corey ran back over to the group after the song and watched them kill the end of the set with Rammstein. The curtain rose again as Korn finished and left the stage. The techs flooded from nowhere to prepare for the final performance.

The massive wave of techs all had Rammstein shirts and began assembling various staging pieces. Lucifer offered a suggestion "Let's get back to the dressing room and have some shots. It's almost that time!" Taylor walked behind the group with Ronan. "Babe" she started. "This is actually happening. I can't believe it" He replied to her "I'm beyond any sort of excitement. Like I'm so excited it's not causing any issues." They both laughed. They arrived back at the dressing room and a woman was waiting with a tray of tequila shots for them. Each member of the group grabbed a glass and raised it. Lucifer laughed and simply said "Hagel den Teufel (Hail the devil)" before drinking his. Everyone else followed suit. Paul gave his best "Wooooooo" again and they headed back to the hallway.

Lucifer stopped Ronan. "Keep an eye out" He said. "I've got some stuff planned for you." Ronan grinned so hard his mouth hurt.

Lucifer and Ronan made their way to the side area just in time to see the other guys getting in place. Flake and Schneider took their places on the stage. Christoph bent over the snare to hide himself as a tech covered him with a black cloth. Paul and Richard stepped onto the light fixtures and strapped their waists in. The platforms began to rise. Lucifer and Oliver remained standing with Ronan and Taylor on the side of the stage as the countdown began on the curtain. The siren sounded off as the curtain dropped and Flake had a red spotlight on him. He started the sequence as Schneider sat up and began his floor tom beat. They played for a few bars before Paul and Richard join in on guitar as they are lowered down amidst a shower of sparks. Once they reach the floor, they ring out a chord and walk off the lights to center stage. Olli ran up to join them jam the hard riff for the next section. Once they finish that riff, they spread out as the lights come down and a spotlight shined onto Lucifer who tap danced in to start their new song, "Rammvier".

A few songs were played before the "Weisses Fleisch" sequence began on the sampler, slow at first, gaining speed. Ronan felt like he was at his peak excitement. Once Richard started his solo, Lucifer came to Ronan and told him "Flake expects you on stage with him at this next part." A shot of panic ran through his body as Lucifer handed him a pair in ear monitors. Schneider started his mini drum solo and stood to dance a couple beats as the keyboard solo picked up. Ronan walked out as Flake came down from his keyboard platform. They looked at each other and nodded as it began. He could hear the sequence and the click track clear as day in his headphones, so it was easy to follow. He danced his best Flake dance, besides the man himself. He had watched him do it for years so had a decent idea of how to give it some justice. Lucifer came back out as the dance ended and fist bumped Ronan as he exited the stage. His legs felt like Jell-O when he got back to Taylor. She was cracking up. "You looked so funny babe, but I guess that's the point so great job!" They finished watching the Rammstein set from side of the stage and Ronan felt like he'd hit a peak of his existence this night. After Lucifer stepped out of his giant metal wings, the band lined up at the front of the stage. He beckoned Ronan to come out with them. The crowd went wild as they bowed for a moment and finally exited the stage.

They regrouped in the dressing room and Taylor stole a quick hug and kiss from Ronan. "This has been magical" She whispered into his ear. He grabbed her and hugged her tight. "It really has been babe and I'm happy you're enjoying yourself too!" Corey and Jonathan walked into the dressing room. "The guys in Avatar are set up with some tunes and booze out in the staging area. Come hang out!" Corey invited them. Lucifer looked around and said to the group "Hell yea. Come out guys. Let's enjoy the peace while it lasts." Rammstein and the kids followed Corey and Jonathan out into the hallway. Ronan saw all the bands congregated in the open area where loads of equipment had been stacked earlier. There is lots of laughing and conversation going on. A loud cheering began when the party realized Lucifer and the kids had arrived. Dani stumbled over as they get closer. "Shots for everyone!" He shouted as John from Avatar brought a bottle of vodka over. They passed

the bottle around before joining the larger group and partied
into the morning hours.

23: THE THULE PRE-WAR POLICY OF ALLIANCE

Ronan woke in his bed. Taylor was next to him. His head was pounding. He lay there, still, for a moment before he remembered the night before. A smile curled his lips. Taylor was on her stomach with her left leg up over Ronan's mid-section. Her beautiful ass was just budding out of the sheet and he ran his hand lightly over her exposed back. He stayed very still, as not to wake her, for a few moments, gently rubbing her back, smiling. He knew evil existed in the world and he felt like they were going to be a part of a big fight but in this moment, his existence was peaceful and full of love and excitement. He gently wiggled his way out from under her. She woke up and rolled over onto her back, exposing her beautiful breasts in the process. He sat on the edge of the bed, admiring the lovely curves of his partner when she spoke. "Last night was amazing. I'm so happy to be here with you. You saved my life." He smiled and placed his hand on hers before he replied, "I couldn't imagine sharing any of this with anyone but you." Banging can be heard downstairs and Ronan smiled. "Mom's making breakfast babe. Let's go get some" He suggested before bending down to give her a very passionate kiss on the lips. He hopped out of bed and scanned for something to wear. Taylor rolled over to his side of the bed and smacked his ass, playfully. "Stop that non-sense or we'll never get out of here" he told her with a smile. "Finnnnnneeeeee" she drew out, smiling herself. She joined him out of bed, looking for something to cover up with for breakfast. She full well planned on having another snack after so she wasn't looking for much to have to remove shortly.

The kids stumbled down stairs to find a busy scene. Emma was cruising around the kitchen as usual. The Reis' were setting the table and dad was nowhere to be found. "Good morning loves!" Emma called out. "Help the Reis' set the table please." They happily helped the couple get some plates and silverware set up for everyone. Emma started placing food on the island and Ronan helped to transfer this food to the table. Sabra asked, "What time did he say the meeting was today?" Everyone gathered around the table to sit and Emma replied, "right around noon time." "Oh good!" He said. "We've got plenty of time to finish up breakfast and clean up then." Everyone sat and began eating. "What is this meeting even about?" Taylor asked. "This battle has been going on for a long time." Karma said. "I think we're looking for a way to finally end it, with the help of you guys." Ronan was deep in thought for a moment. "So, I assume the mission we just completed was to further this cause and the prisoner was key to that?" Ronan thought aloud. "Dad would know" mom told him. "I guess we'll find out together in a few hours!" She said.

As they concluded breakfast amongst talk of the concert, they cleaned up and ventured off from the dining room. Mom told the kids to make sure they're not late to the meeting, and that she'd clean up. Taylor suggested they go find a secluded spot to take a late morning nap and he knew where her brain was at just by looking at her face. He wasn't going to complain about it. The kids said goodbye to everyone and headed out the door. They'd always went to the right which brought you into town, so today they went to the left. Ronan placed his hand on the small of Taylor's back as they walked. She smiled up at him. "I'm curious to see what the end of this road looks like." He told her. "We saw it from the chopper, but I mean, I'm sure it's a different story from down here." "I'm hoping we can find a romantic spot to relax. It's all one waterfall off the side so I want a nice little cove under the water. Some mossy rocks, some privacy…" Taylor trailed off, daydreaming. They came upon a barricade stating the ground was ending. He assumed it said this in other languages he didn't know because there were many other markings on the sign.

He followed Taylor under the barricade and proceeded down a few large rocks to a path of sorts. There was a strong wind and the waterfall was loud but calming. They continued a little way down and Ronan spotted a small opening to the right. He ran over to investigate. Taylor called over to him "Hey babe, it looks like there's a little spot over here, but I don't know how to get down to it." He dropped his head into the hole and saw light. He popped back out and waved her over to him. "Pretty sure this is a tunnel that comes out over there. Let's go check it out!" He helped her down into the hole and they crawled to the other end. It emerged into a wide, mossy spread much like Taylor was describing earlier. He could see the happiness in her face. A small stream of the waterfall ran to a small pool off to the right. "This…is…perfect" she stuttered. Ronan took another good look around and turned back to Taylor who was nearly naked at this point. "Whoa babe! Not wasting any time?" He giggled. She cocked a sexy smile at him. "I'm in love with this place" she told him as she walked around with her arms extended. "I want to enjoy every second here with you" she finished as she approached him. Ronan grabbed her lower back with his left hand and pulled her close. He got a handful of booty in his right hand. "We're going to have plenty of time to do things like this. Years." He tried to comfort her, sensing there was a depression of sorts behind her ruse. She looked up at him. "I don't know" She started. "I've got a bad feeling about what's coming. These are real issues with real consequences if we fail." He kissed her forehead. "Let's not worry until we hear what news the meeting brings." She dropped to her knees and unzipped his dick out of his pants. Ronan took this as a confirmation that she wasn't worrying about it for the time being. She took the whole of it into her mouth and Ronan was once again thankful for all the new and amazing things in his life. He was hiding it well, but he was worried about what was coming too. These next moments were undoubtably going to be very enjoyable, but the meeting would hopefully ease their minds going forward.

The town had started to empty as the auditorium filled up. Shakir was walking toward the building behind a group of Atlantians. Charles wanted to go over a few of the minor details with him and Adam before they would present the plan to the community. He veered off from the flock of people entering the public door as he approached the building. The command center door was around the left side of the building from where he was. As he came around the side of the building, he saw Adam and his team stretching in the field. He was thankful he wasn't late to the meeting. Adam noticed Shakir approaching and called the group to attention. "Great PT team!" He called out "Now go get cleaned up. This meeting is important. Don't be late." Adam picked up his bag and slung it over his shoulder. He met with Shakir by the entrance and they entered together.

The center was very quiet by normal standards, but a skeleton crew was still running the surveillance department. As they approached the center of the room, Charles called out "Just in time comrades! Come. This way" He waved them toward an enclave. Adam dropped the bag behind his desk and the men followed Charles into the room. "Morning guys" Charles said as he gestured them to sit. Charles poured some coffee as Shakir followed Adam to the table and sat. "I've been at this for over 100 years" He began as he placed the coffee on the table and sat himself. "Adam even less. You, Shakir. Much longer. We've grown this operation since we put our collective minds together but we're not making the traction we need. We're spinning our wheels." Shakir piped in. "Well what're you thinking?" Adam was deep in thought. "What's our end game?" Charles simply asked. Adam answered, "Completely get rid of the invaders." Charles nodded "Ok and how have we determined this is possible?" Shakir said "Best case would be to destroy the factory." Charles rubbed his hands together and smirked. "You guys are starting to pick up what I'm thinking. Now, do we know where the factory is?" The men shook their heads in unison. "Who on Earth might know?" Charles asked. Adam slammed his fist on the table shaking the coffee cups. "PIUS" he screamed. Shakir suggested "So I assume then our next mission would be to Rome?" Charles stood. "We're going to end this, once and for all. Let's go get the city on board."

After an amazing hour or so of making love by the waterfall, Ronan and Taylor had fallen asleep on a bed of soft moss. He woke up with Taylor snuggled in closely to him. They were still naked, and it was a very peaceful scene he wasn't ready to disrupt. He'd had many of these recently and he was thankful for all of them. He had a feeling a lot was going to change, and it was coming very soon. Taylor stirred, and he took the opportunity to get her awake. The meeting was happening soon, and he didn't want to be late. He watched her stand up and stayed where he was, drinking in all of her delicious body as she began to dress. Once his daze broke, he also got up to get dressed. Once they were fully clothed, Ronan gave her a kiss and they began back for the road. Once they reached the street, Taylor commented on how empty the city was. "It's a ghost town." Ronan picked up the pace. "Everyone is at the amphitheater. We need to move!" A group of people were still outside the theater piling in when they arrived. Ronan was relieved it hadn't started yet. He brought Taylor around the side and entered the door Shakir had showed them weeks before. The stairs brought them into the control room, but Ronan noted it was much less busy than the last time he was here. A far door opened, and Charles walked out followed by Shakir and Adam. The kids joined the party. "Good morning kids" Charles said. "We're about to start the meeting. Come out with us!" Ronan responded "Ok! Glad we didn't miss it" Shakir showed his signature smirk and Ronan knew what was coming. "Why were you guys late? What were you doing?" He jested. Taylor turned beat red as Adam laughed out loud. "Pay no mind to this one" Charles said. "He is just jealous" He finished before starting to move toward the venue stage. "Let's do this."

The stage was much more formal than it had been for the concert the night before. Some chairs were set up in rows and a fancy podium was in the center of the stage. The theater was as packed as it was for the show, but the people were very calm and ready to listen. Charles approached the podium and began speaking. His voice carried through the chamber. "Friends, family, thank you for coming. As you know, we run our city completely transparent and love feedback on ideas we've got brewing." Adam stepped forward. "Thule, our city is safe from attack due to the advanced cloaking device stolen from the invader's factory. They have since replaced theirs and now we are essentially nonexistent to each other. None of this should be news to you, but the issue becomes that we're unable to locate the factory to launch any sort of attack." Shakir stepped up next. "Our thoughts are now on completely ending this once and for all. We'll need to first find where the factory is hiding. There is only one person on this planet who knows where to find it. We're going to need to extract the Pope." The crowd got loud for a moment. Someone called out from the crowd once it quieted down. "We're never going to be able to get into the Vatican and if we do, we'll never get out alive!" The crowd murmured again. Charles came back to the front and spoke once the room quieted. "We've got a tool this time we've never had before." He turned and beckoned to someone to come to stand with him. Ronan didn't immediately recognize him but as he got closer he got more familiar. It was the Cardinal, Samuel. The crowd stayed silent, waiting for Charles to speak. "This is Samuel. A cardinal from Vatican City." The crowd became very loud. Taylor noticed Samuel looked very uncomfortable. Adam stepped forward and with a booming tone yelled "Thule. You will be respectful." The crowd quieted quickly. Charles continued. "He is as much a victim of the disease as we are. We liberated him, and he has agreed to help us get into the Vatican as a personal favor for helping him escape. He is a brother of ours now and we will treat him as such." Ronan was very in tune with the plan. It made sense. He wasn't sure what the endgame was though. He was just standing by as questions began firing from the crowd.

"How can we be sure the plan will work?" Someone asked from the crowd. Charles answered "We have verified many pieces of information Samuel has provided us. He was very intertwined in Pius' daily life. We're certain the plan will succeed." The man seemed content with the answer and sat down. A woman stood and relayed Ronan's previous thought. "So, what if we get the pope, what is our end game? How are we going to finally end it?" Ronan looked at Taylor, both thinking the same thing; what did she mean by, end it? Shakir stepped forward this time "Yes, we plan to attain the location of the factory and destroy it, along with all of the invaders in one fell swoop." Ronan had more questions but the ruckus starting in the arena held his curious mind. The city was going wild with excitement and he was very interested to be a part of whatever was going to happen.

Charles spoke back up to quiet the crowd. "This is our time. We're to end this madness. For good. It's going to be tough and very messy but prepare for war. Heaven burns. Are you with me?" The crowd erupted with applause. Ronan looked at Taylor. "Heaven huh? Only makes sense it's real and somehow wrapped up in this." Taylor's eyes were lost as she tried to process what she just heard. "We've come this far" She eventually said. "We're going to be the ones to finish it."

24: THE RIGHT TO SELF-DEFENSE

The men met in route to see their father. One had news that needed to be shared and the other needed direction. Michael oversaw security and made sure things went according to plan. His father's plan. He needed direction. Gabriel ran operations and oversaw information flow. He had news to share with his father. The two entered the lift together. "Good morning" Gabriel said to Michael, riddled with distaste. He saw him lost in thought but after a moment, he replied "Morning to you. We'll see how father's mood is today and that will dictate whether it is good or not."

Neither of these men were related by blood to each other and the man they were to see was not the biological father of either of them. These were designations given to them by the organization they worked for and more of a ranking structure than anything. Gabriel found himself able to work with anyone, even if he wasn't a fan of them personally. He was not a fan of Michael. Pompous, arrogant, and moody were just a few of his tamer thoughts about the man. All feelings which were unwarranted as they were ranked the same and Gabriel's performance ranking was usually higher. Others felt the same too, but he was certain Michael had no idea how he felt. He was gifted in seeming neutral to everything but his own musings.

Michael was lost in his head. He had no idea what he should be doing right now and needed his father to tell him what to do. When he had a mission, he did well in completing it. As far as imagination, he lacked immensely. Gabriel, his least favorite brother, had decided to join him this morning. He was always doing his own thing and putting his nose where it didn't belong. The worst of it was he never showed any change of emotion in either direction. Michael acted for reaction and he never got one out of Gabriel. He hated this more than anything.

The lift stopped and Michael reached the door to the throne room before his brother did. He did not hold the door for him either. Gabriel smiled to himself, knowing he'd return the favor someday soon. He stepped inside after Michael and they arrived in the audience chamber together. Their father was not yet there. Michael's impatience showed as he paced and exhaled loudly, like a child. Gabriel patiently had a seat on a stone half wall. After a few moments of watching Michael act like a toddler having a tantrum, the top door opened, and a couple of guards came through with their horns and trumpeted his arrival. Gabriel slowly got off the stone and stood while Michael came to attention where he stood very briskly.

As per usual, it was a hurry up and wait situation. There would be hell to pay should they be late to something, but he showed up whenever he desired. Gabriel was getting bored of standing and waiting for him to show up, so he sat back down. Michael hadn't moved a millimeter and looked like a statue. Their father finally walked through the door and Gabriel noted the look on his face as he stood. He felt like today was going to be one of those days where lots of things died. The old man came down the stairs and plopped his rear onto the throne. He spoke to the men "Come closer my sons. We have matters to discuss." The two moved in to have a more intimate conversation with the old man. Michael tried to talk but the man raised his hand to silence him. Michael didn't look pleased. Gabriel smiled lightly. "Gabriel, what is this urgent news you bring me?" He asked. "Well father" Gabriel began "My ears tell me that an alarming number of the human clergy have been disappearing." The old man clenched his fist and began to turn red. "Lucifer" he grinded out. "I agree father" Michael threw in quickly. "What should I do about it?" Michael asked. The old man stood up. "Thank you for bringing this to my attention Gabriel." Gabriel bowed lightly as acknowledgment. "Michael" He said. "Make ready the ground force. They are up to something and I will not be caught off guard." Michael bowed and departed the room with haste. "I will continue to monitor the situation" Gabriel told his father. "Please do so my son, you're dismissed." Gabriel was happy to leave the room and finish his day at the spa while Michael and his father played war. He wasn't interested in it. Gabriel missed their exiled brother Lucifer. He missed him dearly. They had gone through the academy and come here together all those years ago. He was much more agreeable than Michael had ever been. Treasonous thoughts he kept to himself as he left the throne room.

ABOUT THE AUTHOR

Armin has always had a fondness for world building and creating characters. He began writing stories as early as first grade and has now transitioned into attempting full-fledged novels. Earning extra credit in college by proofreading papers, he strengthened his vocabulary and grammar while helping others submit quality work toward their future. His educational background in business management and marketing has given him a different view to approach many topics in his writing. Armin is happiest when creating which includes writing, music, or photography. A member of three musical acts, he also shoots live concert photography for an online publication. His written reviews of these shows can be found at rockstarculture.com.

www.ingramcontent.com/pod-product-compliance
Lightning Source LLC
Chambersburg PA
CBHW070259120726
47910CB00007B/2311